Infect ME

LAUREN HAMMOND

Edited by Julianne Daly

Cover design by Phat Puppy Art

Interior design by Cait Greer

ISBN - 978-0-9995239-0-2

This one goes out to my lovely students. You guys inspire me on a daily basis. You know who you are.

Chapter
ONE

We're running.

A thousand hands are on me, shoving me in every direction. My fingers are laced through Trevor's, but when a woman to my left elbows me in the gut his fingers slide out of mine and he's being carried away by a swarm of people. It's like we're in a hive. The people have become insects. They are everywhere, their translucent wings fluttering chaotically.

The sound of stomping feet thunders against the pavement. There are men in green military uniforms firing rounds of gunshots into the air. I can hear him, though. I can hear Trevor

1

shouting over the noise. "Keep running, Samara!" He pauses a beat. "Keep running!"

My eyes frantically scan the crowd of people in search of him, but I can't see him anywhere. His voice fades and curls on the wind. He's almost an echo, a voice that I can hear but no longer visualize, and I fear that I've lost him forever.

Hysterical screams, more stampeding footsteps, and sirens blaring from massive tanks parked at the end of the road drown out every other sound. It's impossible to hear anything. I wish I had some earplugs. Industrial earplugs.

More than anything I wish that something could silence the screaming in my head.

I keep running, pushing my way through body after body. I've been running for what feels like lightyears. Where is Trevor? I have to find Trevor. I can't lose him.

He is my love.

He is my life.

The stars don't shine the same when he's not around.

I dodge a woman to my right whose eyes are rimmed in red. Her skin is ashy and translucent. She's been infected and I maneuver away from her as she reaches out to me, crying tears of blood. I will my body to keep going. I pump my thighs harder.

When blood starts raining from their eyeballs, that's when you know to never go near the person. The crimson drops will turn you and twist you into something horrifying. Even the tiniest droplet of red silences your thoughts, mutes your vocal chords, and fries your brain before you become a monster. There are only two ways a person can become infected; by the hemoglobin from another person's veins somehow making its way inside of your body or by a bite.

I can't get near her chompers. Twelve feet is too close, too dangerous, too life altering.

She's going to flip in seconds. Then her mind will switch off and she will no longer be the person crying and reaching out for help. She'll be a robot, she'll be hungry, and she'll want me as a midnight snack.

The CDC was unable to classify the virus when the news of it first broke, but I do remember what the newscaster said as he interviewed someone from the CDC. I sat on my couch, horror etched in my features while the newscaster asked, "How did the victim contact the virus?"

"He was bitten."

"Come again?"

"I said, he was bitten."

Before we had time to even process what was going on with the first victim, the news was reporting a second, a third, and a fourth. Now, it's almost half of the state.

I race ahead and distance myself farther from the infected woman. I glimpse at her from over my shoulder as she buries her head into her hands, still crying. Blood spills out of her cupped hands, branching off at her wrists like a small stream before it flows into the mouth of a river. She can't infect me until she fully turns over to the dark side, and as much as it tears me up inside to see her sobbing and as much as I want to help her, I know I can't.

"Trevor!" I shriek over the howling sirens. "Trevor!"

It's too dark and everyone looks the same. I lost my best friend Chloe when the government officials started ransacking our apartment building and I don't want to lose the only other person I know in this city.

The sirens cut out and up ahead I can see the blockade that consists of men in military uniforms carrying semi-automatic weapons, men in hazmat suits, and tanks more clearly. There's a tall man out in front carrying a megaphone shouting, "Get in line!" His deep voice stretches out, hovering over my head before resting on my shoulders.

I slow my steps. I look to my left. Then I look to my right. I notice that people are forming lines according to gender. The military officials start pushing their way through the crowd aiming their weapons in people's faces, making sure that we fall into formation.

I step to my right and get in line with the women.

As my line moves forward, an announcement blares from one of the speakers on top of one of the tanks. "This is an evacuation! The CDC has declared a global pandemic! Please stay in your line and wait to be evaluated!" Whirling red lights follow the announcement and as they spin, they highlight several of the women's faces in my line. They all seem to look normal, but it always starts out that way. The truth is that any one of them could be infected. From what I've seen on the news, there's an incubation period where the virus lies dormant. It takes anywhere between 48 and 72 hours for the change to begin.

A commotion at the front of my line pulls me from my thoughts. There's a woman crying hysterically while a man in uniform scans her with an instrument that reminds me of a flashlight. There's a glowing, white orb on the end of it that's attached to a narrow metal handle.

The woman continues sobbing and seeing her like that brings a flood of tears to my eyes. Her brown hair rests on her shoulders and moves up and down because she's shaking. She's terrified, I can tell. I'm worried about her—no, not just her. I'm worried about everyone in my line and the men's line.

Gasps, shouting, and cries ring out as the light on the scanner glows bright red and begins beeping. She's been infected. She has to have been. Why else would the light on the scanner change colors?

I'm pretty far back in the line, but the woman's anguished cries reach me, throbbing in my ears. "No!" she wails. "No!" She contorts her body, clawing at the air behind her, reaching for something or someone as she's restrained by two more government officials. She thrashes violently beneath their grasp, trying to use her arms and legs, but the men are muscular, sturdy and strong, and she is far too weak. After a few minutes of struggling, her limbs go limp.

Seconds later, another man in uniform steps forward. My stomach churns and twists as vomit inches its way up my throat. This man is tall, and lanky, but the way he looms over the woman has put the fear of God in her especially when he whips out a gleaming gun. The chrome of the barrel glints against the lighting of a street lamp just to the right of the official and the woman. I swallow hard and gasp as the man lifts the gun, aims it at the woman's head, and pulls the trigger, shooting her right between the eyes. The woman's body curls, slumping over at his feet.

Me, I'm sick to my stomach. My palms begin to sweat. My heart hammers in its cavity. This is not an evacuation.

This is an extinction.

I'm trembling in fear, stunned into silence. Even my mind goes blank. As I take another step forward my knees buckle and I stumble. I can't do this. I can't do this. I know that I'm not infected, but I can't stand here and watch half of these people being massacred. I have to get out of this line.

I start to turn, but as soon as I do, I feel a moist hand clamp over my mouth. Panicking, I stomp down on the person's toe at the same time they drag me out of my line and into a nearby alley kissed by shadows.

A scream gets stuck in my throat and I gag on it. Body heat radiates from the person behind me and bleeds through my clothing. His breaths are shallow and raspy, filling up the canals of my ears. I inhale the musky scent of leather as I roll my eyes to my left. His lips are right next to my ear. A set of full, pink lips, the bottom one just slightly bigger than the top. I know those lips. Those lips have smothered my mouth, kissed every inch of my body, and have whispered loving words into my ears. Trevor's lips. "Stay quiet," he whispers. "Don't make a sound. I am going to get us out of here."

A bloodcurdling shriek pierces the air. I peek around the brick wall of the alley, watching as a rotund man in line charges and lunges forward, attacking a woman with a blonde pixie cut.

Chaos ensues and the lines disband as people start running and screaming in different directions.

That's just the diversion we need.

Trevor grips my fingers and yanks me through the dark alley. We're encased on both sides by red brick building that kiss the never-ending abyss of back sky. I suck in a deep breath as Trevor dodges furniture, garbage, and clothing that's lying against the paved blacktop. His hand is still clamped around mine, so I follow his steps, careful not to trip over anything. Before the evacuation began our homes were torn apart by men in hazmat suits and our belongings were discarded through windows. What baffles me more than anything is how no one knows where this virus originated from, It just showed up one day like a long lost evil cousin and decided to wreak havoc on an entire city.

Trevor picks up speed, sprinting, and practically pulls my shoulder out of its socket. "Trevor! Slow down!" The sirens start howling again. "I can't keep up!"

He lets out a frustrated growl, slows down, and hoists me up over his shoulders. His feet stomp into the ground as he charges forward and my head is bobbing up and down and back and forth. I feel like I'm on a cheap hometown fair ride. I think I'm going to be sick.

I close my eyes to keep the scenery in front of me from spinning and spinning and spinning. When I open them, everything is just a garbled blur and I exhale slowly to eliminate the overwhelming feeling of nausea.

Trevor slows down and I jerk forward as he comes to a halt. He carefully lowers me to the ground while I'm opening my eyes.

We're in front of our apartment building. I stare at the tan brick building with hunter green trellis for a second, thinking of my parents. They paid my rent so that I wouldn't have to live in the dorms. I wonder if they're okay. I can only hope that they are since trying to get a hold of them right now is out of the question.

"Let's go, Mara!" Trevor pulls me toward the side of the building where his Ducati is parked. Once we're at his motorcycle, he gets on, and gives me a hurried look. "Hurry up, Mara! Get on!"

I rush around the side, hop on, and clutch the seat tightly with my thighs. I snake my arms around Trevor's waist, holding on, knowing that if I let go that could very well be the end of me. "Where are we going?" I ask. I hope he has a plan. Then again, it's Trevor. He always has a plan.

Wild howls echo in the distance, followed by a round of gunshots. That tells me officials with semi-automatic weapons are getting closer and they've probably killed at least a dozen more of the infected.

"Some place safe," Trevor says shortly.

Some place safe.

Some place safe.

That seems like an illusion.

A fabrication.

Something made up to keep a child from being terrified of the dark.

After everything I've just witnessed it doesn't seem like that kind of place could exist. I close my eyes and the image of that infected woman being shot in the head flashes through my brain.

It feels like I've swallowed the image and it's now sitting, hanging heavy in my stomach like I've just ingested a bowl of rocks. "But where?"

Trevor revs up the engine to the Ducati, taking off, whizzing through alley after alley and side road after side road. He's doing the right thing. It's probably better if we steer clear of all of the main roads. "Do you trust me?" he shouts over the loud roar of the engine.

"Of course, I trust you!"

"Then can it with the questions, okay?"

He's flustered, I get it. We're in the middle of an extremely tense situation, a life or death situation, but there's no need for snarkiness. "Just tell me where we're going then!"

"To an area where the virus hasn't infected anyone!"

"In the city?"

"Just outside of it."

I trust him, I do, but somehow it seems to me that the place he's talking about couldn't possibly exist. Just last month we watched the outbreak unfold on the news and according to the news and the CDC there's no place the virus hasn't touched.

It is everywhere.

Chapter
TWO

Before

Changes makes me nervous and I don't adapt well to it.

Some people welcome change with open arms, embracing it with all its possibilities. They bask in it, are changed by it. I've always wished that I could be like that. I've always wanted to be able to adapt easily. To just follow suit. Go with the flow. But I can't. Things just don't work that way for me.

So far, I've been in high school for a week and I've been laughed at, shuffled around like a human pinball, and have been given a book job; that's when the upper classmen scamper by and slam their fists onto the mountain of books you're holding. I've been given one four out of the seven days I've been here. The seniors, I've found out, like the element of surprise. When you're just a few steps away from your locker, they swoop up and bam! Suddenly you have a huge mess at your feet. I miss junior high and I never thought I'd ever think that.

Today has moved kind of slow. That might be because it's Friday. It seems to me that the closer I get to freedom for a couple of days, the longer my day drags.

Now, it's fifth period and I stand at the edge of the steps in the cafeteria, my brown lunch bag in my hand as students stroll back and forth between the tables and the lunch line. Loud chatter fills up the room, lined with rows of brown, picnic-like lunch tables. I stand on my tiptoes searching for my best friend, Chloe.

Our story is a typical one. One day in Kindergarten, we were both playing on the playground. I was on the slide and she asked me if I needed a push. We've been best friends ever since, even though we're polar opposites. I'm the quiet, reserved one. She's the boisterous outgoing one. Despite our differences, we have one thing in common - a mutual love for each other - and the truth is that's all we really need.

Crowds of students rush past me, ignoring me. I'm used to being ignored so it really doesn't bother me too much. I'm not a loser, I just keep to myself. I've found that most people ignore the quiet ones. Mainly because we choose not to engage in conversation involving gossip or rumors that spread like an epidemic. She said this. He did that. Honestly, who the hell cares? I have a hard enough time concentrating on what I'm doing rather than worrying about who did what with who and who got totally wasted at last week's party.

I jolt forward the slightest bit as a guy brushes by me. He totally bumped into my shoulder, making me stumble. What the hell? I clutch the wall next to me and steady myself. My eyes widen, and I gawk at the guy. What a freaking jerk. He's half-way across the lunchroom when I realize that he isn't going to stop and apologize. I don't bother saying anything, either. That's one of my biggest problems. I never speak up when I should.

Staring, I take notice in the clothes the guy is wearing. Granted, I can only see him from behind, but I can tell by the faded, worn look of his jeans that they're ripped in the front just below the knee cap. He's wearing a new-looking black leather jacket, and his hair is golden blonde and chin length, glimmering underneath the fluorescent cafeteria lights.

My stomach does a back flip when I notice how proud his walk is. He walks shoulders back, his strides long, like he owns the entire school. He has this air about him. It's impossible to accurately put into words, but I'm mesmerized by him. My eyes drift down to the broadness of his shoulders and I can tell that he definitely has a toned body. With a cocky attitude to match, I'm guessing.

The guy dips into the lunch line, disappearing from my view. I don't even need to see what his face looks like. I can tell just by looking at the back of him that he's a father's worst nightmare.

For a moment, I'm lost in a trance, wrapped up in a daze. I'm staring blankly ahead waiting for the guy to return so that I can catch a glimpse of his face. When he bumped into me, it was so fast that all I could really see were his high cheekbones in his profile.

Movement flashes in my peripheral vision and I snap out of the trance-like state I was in, glancing at a table to my left. Chloe. She smiles brightly, and shakes her head, her auburn bob swishing back and forth.

Walking toward the table, I give her a questioning look as I walk around the table and plop down in the seat across from her. "What?"

"I swear, Samara," she says with a sigh. "Sometimes I swear you live in an alternate reality or something." Chloe's voice is soft and lilting. It reminds me of a lullaby.

"I do not," I protest as I open my bagged lunch and pull out the plastic bag containing my turkey and cheese on wheat.

"You're always staring off like that. It's like you're hypnotized or something."

I'd like to tell her that I'm not Biggie Smalls, but I refrain. I remove my sandwich from the plastic baggie. "No, I don't." I don't always stare off like that. "I just zone out when I'm thinking."

There's a sparkle in Chloe's ocher eyes. "What were you thinking about? Or should I say who were you thinking about?" Chloe likes to play matchmaker. One time in the seventh grade, she set me up with this kid named Marvin. He was all braces, acne, and slobber. Let's just say that was the last time I let her play matchmaker with me.

"Nothing…it was nobody," I mutter as a hint of redness appears on my cheeks. An image of the guy I saw pops into my brain, and I feel like there are sparks going off inside of me, scorching the walls of my stomach.

Chloe shakes her head, our eyes locking. She knows me all too well. I've never been too good at trying to keep things from her; my face gives everything away. "Oh no. That's not a nobody look. That is a somebody look. All right, spill it. Who is he?"

I sigh. I know her. If I don't give her some info she will not let up until, I do. "I don't know."

"What do you mean you don't know?" Chloe places both of her hands flat on the table and cocks her head to the side. "We know every single guy in our grade."

"I don't think he's in our grade. I've never seen him before."

She clicks her tongue, nodding. "Ohhhh. Mara's crushing on an upperclassman."

"I wouldn't exactly call it crushing. First off, he bumped into me and didn't even bother apologizing. Secondly, it's kind of hard to crush on someone you don't even know."

"There's nothing wrong with admiring a little eye candy, my friend."

As soon as Chloe gets the words out I lift my head. Chloe follows my gaze over to the lunch line. There he is—the guy—he's glancing over his shoulder, confident smirk on his lips as he exits the lunch line. My eyes widen, and my lungs clench refusing to expand. I can't breathe. I don't even know this guy and for some reason he manages to assault all of my senses. "That's him," I croak in a soft voice.

"Oh. My. God," Chloe gasps. I glance at her and her mouth is hanging open. "You don't know who that is?"

Of course, I don't. Chloe is the social butterfly of our duo. She makes it a point to know everybody. I'm not going to lie, sometimes she'll walk up to complete and total strangers and introduce herself. By the time she's finished with them, she knows their age, their grade, their likes, and their dislikes.

The guy strolls toward us, a swagger in his step, a devious sexy smirk on his full lips. Just before he turns right to go to his table, he lifts his chin up. Those eyes. Good God those eyes. They are a brilliant blue and gorgeous and just as they pierce my brown ones he says, "What's up?" Hearing his voice nearly cripples me. It's rich and deep and it bounces off my eardrums in the most beautiful way.

I'm singing the words in my mind. They become the most captivating song that I've ever had the pleasure of listening to. *What's up? What's up? What's up?* Oh, God. I can't believe he just spoke to me. He continues walking and I notice that he's wearing a white wife beater beneath his black leather jacket. His rock-hard abs are clearly visible through the flimsy piece of cotton. My eyes trail down the length of his body, stopping at his black combat boots. And I was right about the jeans. They're ripped just below the knee caps.

"He's beautiful," I murmur to Chloe as I get clear look at his heart-shaped face. "Who is he?"

My eyes drift over to him again. He meets my gaze and I can tell by the way he's looking at me that he's analyzing my face. He wears a demure smile, showcasing his row of perfect white teeth, and the sight of it leaves me awestruck. Heat singes my cheeks.

Flustered and nervous, I look down and bite my lip. I don't want him to see or notice how nervous he makes me.

When I lift my head, he's on the opposite side of the cafeteria. He slides into a seat next to Stacia Frost, the captain of the cheerleading squad. Ugh. If he likes girls like Stacia, he's definitely out of my league.

Stacia is only a grade above Chloe and me, but I know firsthand that she's a first-class bitch. When we were in seventh grade and she was in eighth, she used to torment the sixth-grade girls in the band by shoving them in lockers, giving them swirlees, and book jobs. I used to try and stick up for them once in a while when I saw Stacia giving them her best. One time, when I was in the hall on my way to my next class, Stacia had jutted her foot out and tripped a girl in the sixth grade. The poor thing, her books scattered everywhere, and on top of that she face-planted right into the hard wood. It was at that moment that I had had it. I was fuming. Who did this bitch think she was? She started walking away, cackling all the way down the hall when I'd shouted, "Leave her the hell alone, Stacia!"

Upon hearing the words leave my lips her whole body went rigid. She pivoted slowly, anger sparking in her emerald eyes as she stalked straight toward me. "What did you say?" Her voice was low, chilling, and frightening. I froze in my place as she came to a halt two inches from my face.

"I said, leave her alone," I stammered. At the same time my hands were trembling because she terrified me so I hugged my books tightly to my chest to keep them from falling.

A nanosecond later, she shoved me into a locker so hard that I swore I could taste metal in my mouth. Not only that, but the impact knocked the wind out of my lungs. "Mind your own business, you seventh grade maggot!" she shouted as she stormed away from me. I was left with my back to the locker, gasping for air.

Ever since that day, I've avoided her. Well, I've tried to.

Last year was blissfully perfect because while we were still in junior high, she was a freshman in a completely different building. Now, I can see that avoiding her isn't going to be that easy.

Chloe cuts into my thoughts when she leans across the table. "That's Trevor George."

I shoot her a puzzled look. "How do you know him?"

As out of my league as he seems, I'm still curious about him. It occurs to me that most of the guys in school don't look like him.

"I don't know him, know him." She sits back in her seat. "My sister is in his grade. He's new. Rumor is he just broke out of juvie."

So he's a junior. That would make him about sixteen or seventeen. He definitely doesn't *look* like he's sixteen or seventeen. He looks manly and mature and masculine. When he walked by earlier, I could make out a hint of blonde stubble that rests along his angular jawline.

Trevor isn't paying attention so he doesn't know that I'm staring at him. I'm mesmerized all over again and all it took was a flash of his beautiful smile to get me to this point. The point where I'm gazing at him longingly like an adoring fan. The point where even if I close my eyes, I know I'll see his gorgeous face. And when I think of his gorgeous face, my pulse throbs, my breath quickens, and my heart flutters like it's about to fly out of my chest.

Pain strikes my heart when I see Stacia Frost beam at him, flashing her ten thousand dollar veneers while letting out a flirtatious laugh that's loud enough to carry over to my table. I watch as Trevor's hand slips under the table. Immediately my mind goes to places I don't want it to go. In my mind, I see his fingers slowly climbing up her thigh, resting at the place where her black skirt stops. Sighing, I shake my head and try to banish those thoughts from my brain. Stacia giggles again and flips her heavily highlighted hair over her shoulder.

That figures. Hot badass guys like Trevor George always go for girls like Stacia. The confident, bitchy ones who only need to flash one fake smile to get what they want. It's not that I'm not confident. I am. I know who I am. I know that I'm plain, quiet, and prefer ballet lessons and libraries to high school parties. I know that my sense of style is a bit on the simplistic side. I know that I've had more book boyfriends than dates.

And through the years, I've learned something about hot badass guys like Trevor George.

They never go for girls like me.

Chapter THREE

After

There's a tall, dark brown, brick Victorian looking house in front of me.

"How did you find this place?" I ask Trevor as he removes himself from the bike and jogs up the cement porch steps. My vision centers on Trevor's broad shoulders as he turns to the side and barrels into the front door. The door busts open. "Trev?"

He grunts, and lets out a frustrated sigh. He pivots, walking to the edge of the porch, running his hand through his golden locks. "I've been here before. Well not here, here, but I've ridden past this house when I was looking for a place to put my autobody shop. Then earlier when we were separated, I heard a few guys in line talking about this area."

"Are you sure it's safe?" It doesn't feel like any place is safe anymore. "Maybe we should consider leaving the state." From what I know, the outbreak originated in Boston. The news and CDC were very vague when it came to filling people in.

He lifts an eyebrow, giving me a stern look. "Would I bring you here if I didn't think it was safe?"

"No, but we didn't have time to properly assess the situation." It felt like chaos just appeared out of nowhere. No one was given any warning.

He hops down the steps and helps me off the bike. "Look Mara, leaving the state might not be a bad idea, but for right now, it's out of the question. We don't know everything that's going on out there. We have to come up with a plan, gather supplies, weapons. All of that takes time. For right now, we have a safe place to stay. I suggest we take advantage of that and map out a plan after we get situated."

Thinking somewhere is safe isn't good enough, especially in the situation we're in. Knowing, having certainty is much better.

Trevor tilts his head toward the front door. "Come on, let's have a look inside."

He can look inside if he wants to. We haven't even been here for more than ten minutes and I'm already terrified of what might be inside of this house. I gawk up at the brown bricks that have been painted with dirt. Some of the windows on the house are cracked and pieces of glass are chipped off in places. The spouting lining the roof is broken, hanging off in a few areas and if first impressions mean anything, somehow nothing about this house seems safe.

I cast my glance downward, refusing to lock eyes with him. "I don't want to."

In one, swift motion he throws me over his shoulder. "Quit being stubborn. You know I'd never let anything happen to you."

"Put me down, dammit!" I ram my fists into his back, but it's no use. It doesn't even phase him. He continues walking up the porch steps.

He ignores my pleas and sets me down next to the door. "Seriously, Mara. Nothing is going to happen."

But something *did* just happen. "Were you even at the massacre that I was just at?"

An image of the infected woman with bloody eyes fills up my subconscious, and I wish I wouldn't have brought up what I just witnessed. I wish that I could forget everything that just went down somehow, but I know that will never be possible. The memories of all of the infected people and the men with guns will be branded into my mind forever.

Trevor takes me by the hand, leading me through the front door. "I know it's going to be hard to try and forget about everything that just happened." He eyes me then feels around on the wall for a light switch. "We have to move on, though. We have to survive."

21

Days go by.

Then weeks.

Before I even realize it, we've been in our safe house for over a month, but I'm still trying to adapt to our new way of life. Trevor seems to be adjusting just fine, but then again, he's always been the type that accepts whatever curveball the world throws at him and then tries to look at that curveball positively.

I'm sitting on a mattress in the middle of the room counting the canned goods Trevor collected on his last supply run while he boards up the windows and finds a way to bar the door. He makes a supply run once every two weeks. Surprisingly most of the area has been abandoned and that gives us easy access to what the people who have abandoned the area left behind.

We do have a few neighbors left, but we rarely ever speak to them. They mostly stay indoors since the infected population has been growing and growing.

We don't have a television, but we listen to the radio. The broadcasters fill us in on what's going on around us.

Since we've arrived here I've learned that the government lost control of the city. I don't know if they fled the state. I don't know if they just gave up. The radio broadcaster doesn't have all of the answers. In fact, I know that they'll most likely be fleeing soon, and then we'll have nothing.

On top of that, there were a few people that fled from the city that gave us a detailed report of everything that happened since we left. The infected population keeps growing and growing. There are some survivors left, and the ones that remain live in a small village on the south side of the city. A village that's heavily guarded, of course.

I can hear Trevor whistling as he walks through the front door. He seems happy. I don't understand how anyone could find any happiness in this world.

Trevor enters the room, stops whistling, and peers at me from over his shoulder. "You're awfully chipper today," I comment as I pull another can out of the black duffle bag.

"And your point is?"

"I just don't understand how you could be happy at a time like this." Every day is a fight for survival. Every day more and more infected people leave the city and make their way into out neck of the woods.

He chuckles and makes his 'I'm thinking face' where he scrunches his eyebrows together and rests his thumb and forefinger against his chin. "Why shouldn't I be?"

Normally, when he agitates me, I eventually break and start giggling. But not now. Not today. "Trevor, stop." My voice is strained yet at the same time loud and forceful.

He gives me a sympathetic look and the mattress dips down when he sits down next to me. "Mara, stop being like this." He reaches up and tucks a piece of my hair behind my ear. The feel of his fingertips sends a rush, a thrill, a jolt throughout my entire body. It's crazy how just one little swipe of his finger can make me feel like a live wire just came in contact with my body. Suddenly, I become a masochist, yearning and eager for the pain that he's about to inflict. "I know the world has gone to shit."

Shit is an understatement. The world has been fucked. Royally.

Sometimes when I look at Trevor, the only thing I can visualize is that last moment right before Trevor plucked me out of my line. The moment when the government official shot the infected woman in the head. The moment when her body slumped over, smacking into the pavement like a bag of wet sand; heavy, dead weight.

Trevor envelopes me in his arms. I snuggle closer to him, tucking my head underneath his chin, and pulling my legs up into his lap. The sound of his heartbeat pounds in my ears as I place my head flat against his muscled chest, and the warmth of his body sends an overwhelming calmness swirling through me. I slide my fingers up his arm, playing with one of the straps of his wife beater. "I wish I could be more like you," I tell him. "I wish I wasn't so negative."

He plants a soft kiss on the top of my head, sighing. "I can understand why you would be negative. There's nothing good left in the world. People are infected with a virus that has no cure. They die and eat each other or wind up murdered, put down like an old horse. But it's like I said before; as long as we stick together, stay on our toes, and keep our eyes open, we will be fine."

I smile but it doesn't touch my eyes. "I hope you're right."

"I am, love." He places two fingers underneath my chin, titling my head up. He beams at me and when he smiles his whole face lights up. His cheeks glow, his eyes gleam. He's even more beautiful than usual when he's like this. Like when he's so happy that it trumps every other emotion.

Trevor is one of those people who is guarded, but if you take one look at their face you'll know exactly how they're feeling. That's one of my favorite things about him. "I know I'm right."

I stare into eyes.

There's an earnest look residing there.

He believes this.

He believes that we'll be okay.

I want to believe that too.

So, the only thing that's left for me to do is to take his word for it.

Chapter
FOUR

Before

It has been three weeks since the first time I saw Trevor George, and I haven't been able to stop thinking about him.

When I close my eyes, I see his face, his sharp strong features, and his beautiful sapphire eyes. His deep, melodic voice plays in my mind like a concert pianist performing his rendition of *Moonlight Sonata*. I even imagine his hands on me sometimes. The warmth from his skin bleeding through mine. Butterflies flap their wings against the walls of my stomach whenever I envision physical contact with him. Just thinking about it makes me shiver.

Believe me, I've tried to deter myself from thinking about him, but nothing I do seems to work.

At lunch, I switched seats with Chloe so that my back would be to him, but it was no use. My eyes would find him when he was walking back from the lunch line and they would find him when I'd occasionally sneak a peek from over my shoulder. In between classes I'd run straight to my locker, avoiding any hallway chit-chat, grabbing my books in a hurry so that I didn't just happen upon him while he was making his way to his next class. That didn't work either. Two days ago, I ran into him— no, not just ran, collided. Upon impact, my books flew up into the air and papers from my folders flew up into the air, cascading down like little snowflakes that were mere inches away from dotting the ground before a white out.

"Sorry," I muttered as I hurriedly scooped my papers. I kept my head down hoping that he wouldn't see the ripe tomato color of my cheeks.

Trevor crouched down in front of me, but I couldn't bring myself to look at his face. "Here," he said. "Let me help you." I kept my eyes on the floor, watching as his long fingers skated across the polished wood, sweeping up all of my books in one swift motion. He stood slowly, holding my books out to me. I hesitated, still on the floor, my eyes planted on his big, black combat boots.

My stomach was in knots.

What should I say?

What could I do?

I needed to time to come up with something to say.

The problem was that I didn't have any.

I exhaled, swallowed, made a mental note to act cool. Then I stood up to face him.

"Thanks," I said, trying as hard as I could not to look at his face. My eyes fixed on the tan metal locker behind him. But then, I took my books from his hand. The second my skin brushed against his, something sizzled inside of me. My heart started racing. My breaths became short, and raspy. I couldn't believe that all it took was one, simple touch to make my insides come alive with want. There was something between us, I could feel it. Deep down inside I wondered if he could feel it too.

"No problem," he answered.

I was speechless. Torn up inside. Ripped apart at the seams. I never spent a lot of time conversing with boys. Don't get me wrong, I wasn't a total wallflower; there were times when I tried. Like in junior high, there were a few boys, but I always wound up saying the wrong thing or, even worse, when they tried to talk to me my mind would go blank and I wouldn't say anything at all.

I met Trevor's gaze for a second, saluted him, then mentally cursed myself for doing that. What the hell was I thinking? Yes, you idiot, you just tossed him a salute, like military style you moron. You just saluted one of the hottest boys in school. You're a real winner, Samara, a real winner.

He stared at me, puzzled. He wore a cocky smirk as his baby blues scanned my face. I'd been given that look before. That this-nutjob-has-a-major-crush look.

Embarrassed and eager to excuse myself from the awkward situation, I grunted a goodbye at him, rushing down the hall to my next class.

Yesterday at lunch, I saw him getting awfully chummy with Stacia and it was at that moment that I knew that what I thought I had felt in the hallway between us was just my mind playing tricks on me. I had to remind myself that Trevor was probably just being nice by helping me with my books and that he would always be out of my league.

Chloe sits down across from me, and her bright smile pulls me from my thoughts. I smile back, pulling a banana out of my lunch bag. "What is it?" There's a mischievousness to Chloe's smile that tells me that something is up.

"Someone is starting at you."

I don't want to play games with her – I never do. "Huh?"

She nods slyly to her right. "Have a look."

I peer over my shoulder and before I have the chance to even meet his gaze, I can feel Trevor's eyes on me. I look away bashfully, but not before noticing the scowl on Stacia Frost's face. A triumphant flutter flits through my stomach and I smile to myself. So maybe he doesn't like girls like Stacia. All I know is that that look on her face is priceless.

Blushing, I peel my banana and take a bite. "Looks like you have an admirer," Chloe muses.

"Stop it," I tell her, waving her off, my mouth full of chewed up fruit.

Chloe giggles. "Lucky you. I bet Stacia wishes that he was gawking at her like that right now."

I know she does.

"So, he's looking at me." I try to play it off casually even though I feel my heart pounding, slamming into my ribcage, and my stomach is doing several back flips. "Big deal."

I lower my head, and Chloe looks at Trevor again, shaking her head. "That boy is too hot for his own good." I keep my eyes on my brown lunch bag, and feel the pull of a smile on my lips. Maybe he's not as out of my league as I thought.

At the end of the day, I wait by the back steps of the school for my mom to come pick me up. I never have to wait long because she's almost always right on time. My mom has this thing about being punctual. She considers tardiness a character flaw. I find this comical because my dad is never on time for anything. Whenever we go anywhere, she and I are usually waiting for him.

"For the love of all that's holy, Dale what could you possibly be doing up there?" She'd shout at him. Dad is one of those people that has to have every strand of hair in the proper place. If it takes him a little longer to get ready, then so be it.

Bright, radiant sunlight beams down from the heavens. The heat from the sun sizzles against my ivory skin. Glancing around, I try to look for a spot of shade, but I don't see any. I know there are some people who love basking in the sunlight, but I'm not one of those people. Besides, my skin only has two shades and that's white and pink.

Sitting down on the cement steps, I feel the burn and can tell that I'm getting pinker by the minute. I close my eyes, inhaling the fresh air. The gentle hum from an engine purrs in my ears, and when I open my eyes, Trevor is in front of me, revving up the engine of his Ducati.

The sun hits the silver paint job, and the bike sparkles and gleams. Anxiety whooshes through me, and my jaw locks as Trevor yanks off his helmet, runs a hand through his hair, and cocks his head to the side, wearing a devilish grin. "You're Samara Moore, right?"

"Er...Um...Sure," I stammer, fighting to find the right words. I wish that his presence wouldn't always make me feel so flustered. Talking to him is too nerve-racking, too complicated. Admiring him from afar is much easier.

"You have fifth period lunch, right?"

"I do," I say softly, blushing. "So do you." I choke on my previous comment. "I mean I think you might. I mean I think I might have seen you in there a couple of times." I am so nervous that I'm totally screwing up the first real conversation that we've ever had. On top of that, he intimidates me with his perfect smile, bulging biceps, and hard, yet gentle, demeanor.

I expect him to think that I'm crazy. Like an obsessed fan chasing after her celebrity crush thinking that she has a real shot at a relationship. But Trevor surprises me. In a flash, he chucks the spare helmet at me, and I shock myself when I catch it. Sure, I take ballet, and I can be graceful, but when it comes to being athletically inclined I am severely lacking. I can't even dribble a basketball in gym class.

He crooks me a wickedly beautiful grin. "Want to go for a ride?"

For a moment, excitement blows up inside of me. I feel like I just played the best carnival game ever and all I want to do is hop up and claim my prize. Then my heart sinks like an iron anchor, plummeting to the ocean floor. "I can't," I say, tossing the helmet back at him. When he catches the helmet, depression swirls around inside of me, oozing out through my voice, "My mom is picking me up. She'll be here any minute."

He nods and fastens the helmet onto the side of his bike. "Then maybe we could try this again sometime. Like say, Friday at 7:00 p.m."

"I'd like that." I'd more than like that. I'd love that.

"Good." Trevor winks at me, puts his helmet on, and speeds through the parking lot.

Me, I stand and start jumping up and down giddily. I even do a little happy dance. As my mom pulls up in her mini-van, I replay several different scenarios in my mind of me getting her to agree to two things; one, to let me go on my first date with a slightly older guy, and two, convincing her to let me ride on the back of his Ducati.

Chapter FIVE

After

The sky is raining bullets and it's almost like the metal punctures a hole in my heart. Blasts from shotguns hang in the air like the echo of a song.

I stand at my window, peeking through the blinds as the thick dust wafts up from the crème plastic and floats into my eyes. An incessant ache clutches onto my side, and squeezes tightly as I watch our neighbors being slaughtered.

Radio coverage has cut out altogether. The last I heard was that more and more of the infected were migrating toward us. Then the broadcaster signed off saying the surviving population was on their own.

I watch a man from the window as he kicks a body on the street, checking to see if they're still alive.

Despicable Renegades. Or at least that's what they like to call themselves. Trevor has conversed with them a few times, and while he thinks they're doing us a favor, I think they're stupid.

They ride in here on their motorcycles thinking that they're saviors on white stallions. They think that murdering the infected people can save humanity. They are fools. Humanity is lost. A car key buried beneath a mountain of white snow. It can never be found. It can never be saved.

Two months.

We've been in our safe spot for two months.

And all the renegades are doing are murdering people and attracted more infected to the areas where the uninfected people are hiding.

They thrive on noise, the infected.

It attracts them.

Fuels them.

So far, Trevor and I have kept a low profile, managing to stay under the radar. Now, the idiot Renegades on a power trip are ruining it.

There were several of the infected that made it out of the massacre in the city. It took them a few weeks, but they eventually made their way to us. We had a little bit of warning from the broadcasters on the radio, but not enough. Before we had time to process everything they were here, infecting our neighbors.

The Renegades' headquarters is on the other side of the city, but they come here to make supply runs. That's probably because when everything started happening this area was safer than anywhere else. Not long after that, they started making weekly patrols.

Another loud blast fills my ears as a tall, burly male renegade with a vengeance fires his shotgun, putting a bullet between Mrs. Walter's eyes. She lived three houses down from us. There's a small part of me that understands what they're doing, but at the same time there's an even bigger part of me that wishes that they would just mind their own business.

A blank, lifeless expression crosses over Mrs. Walter's features as blood dribbles down her forehead and branches off at her nose. Even though she's dead, when I gaze into her cold, emotionally deserted eyes I feel like she's looking right through me, staring straight into my soul.

I feel like her empty puddles of blue are telling me that it's only a matter of time before I'm infected too.

Tortured howls and wails echo through the air as more of the renegades fire holes into people's skulls. Hysteria unfurls in the pit of my stomach like smoke coiling up from a fireplace and as three more bodies drop, I back away from the window. Infected or not, I can't handle seeing more people die today.

I walk backwards as the moonlight bleeds through the separations in the blinds, filling the room with a dim glow. Then I plop down on the ratty, bare mattress in the center of the room. Fear oozes through my pores and infiltrates my bloodstream when I think of how close I am to death.

It lives right outside of my door.

It seems like every day another neighbor becomes infected. It has only been three months since the carrier of the virus was discovered in the area, and it's crazy to me how it only took three months for the outbreak to escalate even further.

More people scream. They are begging and pleading for their lives, and their anguished cries strike a nerve in me. Tears flow from my muddy brown eyes like the Nile. Rushing water with a fast current. I sob. I sob so hard that I'm having trouble breathing. I'm an empty oxygen tank. I hope someone fills me up soon.

Most of all, I'm sick with worry because Trevor is out there. He's outside in a world that's filled with death and destruction.

There are piles of rotting bodies on the corners of the streets. The rotting stench of decayed flesh seeps in through the cracks in the walls, and permeates the air. The smell leaves me feeling uneasy, and a million questions travel through my brain. What if he's one of them? I hate to say it, but I have to consider it. What if Trevor has been infected? If he has been infected I hope he comes back for me.

And I hope that he infects me too.

I've loved Trevor hopelessly and irrevocably since I was fourteen years old. I've loved him with every flicker of my soul, and I will continue to love him until I take my last breath.

The first words Trevor ever spoke to me always linger in the back of my mind accompanied by a flash of his image, his beautiful, cocky smirk, and the sly way he runs his fingers through his stands of gold. "What's up?" They aren't the most memorable words, but the way Trevor's deep rich voice sounded when he said them reminded me of hot creamy chocolate being drizzled over fresh strawberries. Point blank, his voice is delectable enough to eat.

And the way he said them….

The words….

The way he said them made me feel like he was prying deep inside of me to get the answer, an answer I was unable to give him at the time.

"Samara." Trevor's hushed voice pulls me out of my reverie, and I hop up from the bed, rushing to meet him at the front door. He drops a backpack from his shoulder and it thuds against the floor as he secures the bolted lock on the front door. Then he faces me, tucking his chin-length hair behind his ears with a wide-toothed grin on his face.

I crash into his arms, inhaling the musty scent of death and decay. I don't care that he stinks. I don't care that he has splotches of dirt on his toned, muscled arms. All I care about is that he's home, that he's safe, and that he's not infected.

Or is he?

I lower my gaze, noticing a spot of blood on his wife beater just above his six pack that protrudes through the flimsy cotton. I feel his eyes on me. His staring burns a hole right through my skin, and panic whips through me like a hurricane. Trevor pulls me close, and kisses the top of my head. He knows what I'm thinking. "Calm down, Mara. I haven't been infected."

Looking up into his eyes, I search the pools of blue for answers. "The blood?"

"I had to shoot one."

Relief whooshes through me, and I relax beneath his firm grip. "You had me terrified," I tell him. He leaves all the time while I'm stuck at home with nothing to do but worry. "I thought something happened to you." I plant kisses all over his face. "Don't ever leave without me again." I plant a long, lingering kiss on his full lips.

When he left two hours ago to go look for weapons and supplies we got into an argument because I wanted to go with him.

"Trevor, please," I begged. The thought of me staying behind while he went off in search of supplies didn't feel right. "I know I can help!"

"You won't be helping me, Mara. You'll be distracting me. I won't be able to focus on the task at hand if I'm too busy worrying about you. Just stay here, and don't make a sound. I'll be back soon."

Him leaving me was worse than me going with him. He was gone for over three hours, and the uncertainty of the situation gnawed at my insides. It infuriated me that he just expected me to sit at home and wait.

Or panic.

You never know what the infected have in store for you. It's like being given an ugly sweater for Christmas every year; you don't want it, but you can't control what you get. I wish I could control the infected. I wish that there was some magical remote somewhere with a red pause button that allowed me to freeze them in place. Halt. Don't move. You don't really need to gnaw on that forearm, do you? That way, every time Trevor leaves, I wouldn't have to wonder if they bit him or—even worse—if he was dead.

Trevor distracts me from my thoughts when he cups my face. Suddenly I'm drowning in pools of blue. I don't need to breathe. Who needs air when you're captivated by something so beautiful? "You know I have to leave every now and then to look for things we need: food, guns, fuel, clothes."

"Next time I'm going with you." I put force behind my words to make my point.

"Just stop it, Mara. You can't. It's too dangerous."

"I'm. Going. With. You."

He silences me, his lips fluttering gently over mine. My whole body is on fire for him. My heart hammers into my ribcage, and my fingers tremble as I try to clutch his arms. I can't imagine my life without him. I can't imagine what I would do if he became infected and I lost him. Trevor is the only reason I have survived this outbreak.

I rest my forehead against his. Then I slide down, placing my head flat against his chest, listening to the gentle strum of his heartbeat. The rhythmic thumping silences my thoughts, calms my nerves, puts me at ease. "I don't care what you say," I tell him. "Next time I'm going with you."

"We'll see about that." There's a smile in his voice.

Trevor always has to be in control. He's always the alpha. Always swooping in to save the day. My own personal hero.

But what he doesn't know is that if I have to become a contortionist and squeeze myself into that tiny little duffle so that I can be of some help, I will do it.

All I want is for him to let me do something, anything. I'm so sick and tired of feeling like I'm absolutely useless. Sometimes it infuriates me that he wants me to stay inside the house all of the time while he goes out and risks his life to make sure we have what we need. Once, just once, I wish he would let me be the one that puts my life on the line for him.

I know that when the time comes for him to go out again that there will be a fight.

But next time...

Next time I know that I will be the one who wins.

Chapter SIX

Before

When I was a little girl, my grandmother looked at me on my third birthday and said, "Sweetheart, before you know it, your life is going to just fly on by."

At the time I didn't pay much attention to what she said, but as I stand in front of my mirror at seventeen, I can't believe how right she was.

I also can't believe that Trevor and I have been together for three whole years. We went from awkward first dates to being a seasoned couple overnight, I swear.

Trevor lies back on my bed, a stress ball in his hand. He crosses his ankles, tosses the ball into the air, and catches it.

LAUREN HAMMOND

I stand in front of my mirror, smoothing my long black hair into a bun, securing it on the top of my head with a few bobby pins. I lock eyes with Trevor through the mirror, a smile curling on my lips. I don't think I'll ever get over the feeling of desire that courses through my veins whenever I'm near him. It's like my mind and my emotions are in sync with one another. There's no need for a war between them. They know what love is. True, pure incandescent love.

Out of the corner of my eye, I see him wink at me. There are flames in my cheeks, a skip in my heart beat, and sweaty palms galore. You would think that after three years that he wouldn't still make me flustered, but he does.

Wandering over to my bed, I brush against the frilly pink comforter, and pick up my duffle bag. My room is so child-like with its pink walls and white trim. I guess my parents never understood the idea of a child outgrowing their room because mine has been exactly the same since I was born.

I walk over my closet, reach inside my shoe rack, pick up my pointe shoes, and then I unzip my duffle bag, stuffing them inside. I've been taking ballet since I was three years old. I attend classes three days a week in the evenings after school.

Ballet is life.

When I was little, I never really took it seriously. I just figured it was something that I could do with my life, almost like a leisurely activity. And recitals, well, they were always fun. It wasn't until junior high that I really became devoted to it. I'd eat, sleep, and live ballet. I was always anxious to attend every class, never missing a day.

Every year since I was six years old, my mom took me to see The Nutcracker. It was a ritual of ours. The Nutcracker always came to town right around Christmas. And my mom, she always made a big to-do of it all. We'd get dressed in our best clothes, go out to dinner at some fancy restaurant, and then we'd watch the pretty ballerinas as their bodies became one with the music, and a story was told through dance in front of our eyes.

There was always a thrill that went through me whenever I saw the dancers perform. When I was twelve, I looked up at my mom, excitement shimmering through my chocolate brown eyes and I said, "One day that's going to be me up there. One day, I'm going to be Clara."

Mom had always been supportive. She always believed that I could reach for the stars, pluck one from the sky, and hold it in my palm. "That's a wonderful ambition to have, sweetheart."

It's not just an ambition anymore.

After fourteen years of hard work, passion, and dedication, I've finally done it. I've landed the part of Clara. Tonight is the dress rehearsal. Tomorrow is the first show.

"You know you don't have to come," I tell Trevor as I zip up my duffle and swing it over my shoulder.

The truth is that I want him there more than anything, but at the same time I don't want to be that demanding girlfriend that always makes her boyfriend do things that he doesn't want to do.

Trevor drops the stress ball and sets it down on my bed. "Are you kidding me? I'd be the world's most terrible boyfriend if I wasn't there for my girlfriend's moment of glory."

Even though he says he's going to come and see me, I'm not going to hold my breath. Trevor is the gruff, manly type. I know he's rather sit around with his buddies, chugging beers and working on his bike while watching football. I can't even count the little tiffs we've gotten into because of all the chick-flicks I pick out every time we go to the movies. "But if you don't, I'll understand."

I start for the door, and Trevor meets me halfway. He grazes his fingertips against my cheek, smiling at me lovingly. "I'll be there, I promise." He plants a soft kiss on my cheek and opens the door for me.

The next three days go by in a blur. There is a show Friday, Saturday, and Sunday and after at least a dozen costume changes, twenty-four makeup applications, and forty-eight leaps, I am doing my final pirouette on stage in front of a packed auditorium.

Trevor didn't show for the first two performances, but he did send sweet texts before each show.

I know you'll be amazing. Call me after the show.

Knock em dead, love.

I complete my pirouette, throw my hand up in the air, and prepare to bow. I hesitate briefly, my eyes sweeping over the crowded auditorium as people get to their feet and roar with applause. A bright smile stretches across my lips, and my heart leaps like a tour jeté when I see Trevor in the third row, on his feet, bringing his fingers to his lips, whistling.

After the show, Mom makes us huddle together for a picture. She holds her Canon close to her chest, her black bob bouncing as she moves her arm. She's always been a little camera happy. I guess that has a lot to do with me being her only child. "All right, Trevor," she says. "Put your arm around Samara."

Trevor slides his arm around my shoulder while I stare up at him, gazing into his eyes. He came. He came. He came. Of course, I had my doubts, but the I had secretly hoped that he wouldn't let me down. "You came."

He kisses my forehead. "Of course I came. I told you I was going to, didn't I?"

"Yeah, but I…."

"Mara, when I give you my word, I mean it." We both face my mom. She lifts the camera to her right eye and squints her left one. "You should know me by now," Trevor says. "I never break my promises to you."

This is true. Any time I've ever needed him he'd always be there and I now I think that it's silly that I ever had doubts in the first place. "Thanks, Trev. It means a lot to me that you came."

"Say cheese," Mom says with a smile.

We both smile, and for a second I wonder if my Mom can see the love in our eyes. I wonder if she realizes that Trevor is it for me. That I'll never love another the way that I love him. I wonder if she can see the same thing radiating from his eyes. I don't even need to look at him, and I know.

I steal a glance at Trevor. He's beaming, his smile brilliant and beautiful. He looks so happy. I hope he stays that way forever. I hope that nothing in the world could ever turn his blue-sky gray. Those are the things I want for him, my love, my life.

I eye my mom.

She nods.

Then we're both blinded by a series of flashes.

Chapter SEVEN

After

My dreams are the only thing that I have that are sacred anymore.

After I close my eyes, I know there will be no more hurt. There will be no death. My dreams take me to a place of happiness and love and they are full of beautiful memories from my past. The years before the outbreak.

A demure smile spans across my lips when I think of sleep, and how for years I fought with my parents over my bed time. My parents. Sadness bubbles inside of me like joining water when I think about them. I haven't spoken to my mom since right before the news of the outbreak broke. From that moment on, everything happened too quickly—too fast. One day our home was being strip-searched, the next day we were running for our lives. Amidst the chaos, even though I wanted to, I had no time to call in and check on my parents. Questions bounce around my brain on a daily basis. What if they tried to call me? What if they're infected? What if they're dead? The sad reality is that I don't know what happened to them, and I don't know if I ever will.

Trevor and I lie down on the bare mattress. He covers me with his leather jacket as he softly kisses my neck. "Sleep tight, my love," he whispers, wrapping one of his strong arms around my waist. His warm breath trails down my neck as he breathes into my hair.

He fills me up with so much love and happiness that I feel like I'm about to explode. "I was so worried about you today," I murmur, feeling exhaustion set in. My eyelids droop down and Trevor's soft breathing fills my ears.

Most of the time, I wish we still had our cell phones. I know that during these dire times that that's a silly thought to have, right? Screw survival. I vote for modern technology. But somehow having my cellphone, knowing that Trevor would be able to contact me when he goes out on supply runs makes me feel better. I swallow the thought. Three months ago, we were shuffled out of our homes by government officials with guns and gas masks. We were forced to leave everything behind.

"You don't need to worry about me, Mara," Trevor says. "I'll always be here for you. I'll never leave you." Even though he says that, I know that's not necessarily true. I bet the loved ones of people in our neighborhood said the same exact thing, and the next day they wound up infected. Trevor kisses my hair and whispers, "It will always be you and me against the world."

He sounds so confident when he tells me that; you and me against the world.

And the last thing I think about before I drift off to sleep is that I wish I could believe him.

The rattling begins around midnight. A rattling so intense that it makes every dusty, old picture on the wall shake. It's like the infected are attracted to the night. The stars become sirens, hypnotizing them, and guiding them to the only humans left in this area.

Terror rips through the lining of my stomach, and I think I'm going to be sick. My eyes fly open, and I bolt upright, dry heaving. I bite down the nauseous feeling as the fists of the infected echo into the house. I listen to their moans, their incessant cries of hunger. They crave, want, need flesh. My flesh.

I place my head in my hands, sobbing softly. I keep my cries barely above a whimper, hoping that I don't wake Trevor. I hastily wipe my tears, peeking at him through the tiny gaps in my fingers.

In this grim world, he lights up the darkest of days. He reminds me of what life was like before the virus broke out. Happy and fleeting. We never had to worry about whether or not we'd be eaten or—even worse— turned into murderous monsters who gnawed at the arms and legs of human beings, cleaning off tendons with their sharpened teeth.

Trevor is so beautiful when he sleeps. His chest rises up and down, in sync with his short breaths. His breathing sounds like a rhythmic sonata orchestrated by a symphony. I focus on his long, dark lashes, and exhale.

I've always found peace in watching Trevor sleep. Before and after the outbreak. We'd lie in bed and I would prop my head up with my elbow, staring. Captivated by the beauty of his peach skin, long lashes, and flaxen blonde hair. When I watched him, he seemed to dive deeper and deeper and deeper into a world of love and serenity, a world that I was elated to accompany him to.

Sometimes he would only pretend to be sleeping. After a few minutes, a cocky grin would spread across his lips. Then he'd grab me by my small waist, hoist me up over top of him, and brush my bangs away from my forehead. "Sneaky, sneaky," he'd say with a laugh. "What's the appeal in watching me sleep?"

"You remind me of peace," I'd answer. "Like every problem in the world has dwindled away."

My thoughts are interrupted when the rattling against the house grows louder. Fear spins around inside of me like a cyclone on a path of destruction as it rips through the Midwest. On top of that, I feel like a rat trapped in a cage. All the doors are barricaded with locks and wooden planks and makeshift metal bars are welded across the windows. But still....

I feel like it's only a matter of time before I'm yanked out of this cage. Soon the scientists will put me out by my fleshy tail and shoot me up with needles and various drugs just to see my reaction.

I yelp, terrified, and lie back down, trembling. A moment later Trevor's arm slips over my waist, pulling me closer to him. I twist to the side and find his blue eyes in the dark. His eyes, they're as bright as a sparkling sapphire. A tear drizzles down my cheek. I wipe it away quickly, but as soon as I do more start pouring from my eyes.

Trevor leans over, kissing the tear away. "Don't cry, Mara."

I never used to cry this much, but then again my life never used to hang by a thread the way it does now. "I can't help it."

I feel like every day that I live might be my last.

A loud boom comes from the front door, and I jump, gasping out. Trevor grips my waist tighter, sliding his hands up my body. His lips touch my ear. "Shhhh, love. You sleep." Then he presses his hands over my ears to drown out the sound of the moans and rattling. He does this every other night. He knows how bad the noise from the infected frightens me. He's always willing to sacrifice sleep so that I don't have to.

There have been many times where I've tried to fight him, telling him that he needs the sleep more than I do, but he always insists and I wind up agreeing just to save us from having a squabble. I wish that I could be more like him, so selfless and brave. I think about one time where he barreled through a group of the infected without even getting a scratch on him.

It was only a month and a half after we'd moved into our new place. I watched him through the window as he was being surrounded by monsters with blood dripping from their lips.

Panicking, I flew out the front door. I started down the porch steps, running for him. I came to a sudden halt when he shouted,

"Don't you dare come any closer, Mara!" His words were followed by a finger to his lips.

Keep quiet.

Be still.

I mean it, don't utter a peep.

I felt so torn. I couldn't just stand there and do nothing. I couldn't watch in horror while the love of my life was being chewed to bits by a pack of ravenous human-like hyenas.

What happened next took me by surprise. One moment he was surrounded and the next there were a bunch of the infected struggling to get to their feet. There were some kicks, punches, a few elbows to the gut, and it all happened so fast. Before I could move he was running toward me, yanking me by the arm back into the house.

"Trevor, I…" I had no words.

After we made it back into the safety of the house, and locked and barricaded the front door, he looked at me sternly, and said, "Don't you ever try that again."

Baffled, I gawked at him. "Try, what?" What the hell did he think? Did he think I was going to just stand there and let him die?

"Being a hero, and running to my rescue."

"I couldn't live in this world without you. I wouldn't survive it," I told him, meaning every word of it.

He smiled. "I doubt that, love. I think you've got some fight deep down inside of you somewhere."

I tuck that flashback into a corner of my brain when Trevor shifts in bed next to me. "But what about you?"

He shakes his head. "Don't worry about me. I'll be fine."

"But…"

He kisses my temple, removes a hand from my ear, and whispers, "Just sleep, love." His voice is muffled as he presses both of his hands on my ears harder. Then I drift off into a land where nothing and no one can hurt me. I dream. I dream of happy and beautiful moments from my past.

"Good Morning, beautiful." Trevor's voice fills up every part of me. I hear him in my head, in my ears, and in my heart.

I exhale as he clutches on to me tightly. "I'm sure beautiful is way too much of an overstatement." Even I'm frightened of my own reflection when I stare at it first thing in the morning. Sometimes I have bluish black circles under my eyes. Sometimes my hair sticks up in various directions. It's a hit or miss kind of thing.

Trevor hovers above me, smelling clean, like fresh water mixed with Dove soap. I roll over, facing him. He tucks a strand of my hair behind my ear before placing a soft kiss on my forehead. My eyelids flutter, and I gaze into his melted sapphire blues that are only an inch away from my face. "Did you sleep at all last night?" I ask, concerned.

"Some," he answers me in a soft voice. I know he's lying. He's like a hardass who lies about the pain that accompanies a broken bone. Oh, it's nothing. Nothing at all, I swear. He's always trying to make things seem less than what they really are. When he says he got 'some' sleep, that means he didn't get any.

I frown. "Why don't you try to go to bed?" I sit up. "I'm going to go shower."

He folds up his arms, nestling them in behind his head. "But it's so bright out. You know I can't sleep during the day."

I stop on his side of the bed, and lace my fingers through his. "Just try for me. Please. I'll feel better if you do."

"Fine," he sighs, defeated. "But only because I hate to see you upset." I try to pull away from him, but he lets out a soft laugh, yanks on my arm, and playfully clutches my waist before pinning me down on the bed.

His fingers glide up my shirt, and wander over my stomach as goosebumps rise all over my skin. He's half on top of me, and my knees go up instinctively as his fingertips dig into my stomach. "Stop it," I giggle. "That tickles." He crushes his lips to mine, brushing his tongue over the tip of mine. Then he backs out of the kiss, falling back on the bed. The feeling I experienced when he kissed me was euphoric. I'm disappointed that it's over. I pop myself up on my elbows, frowning. "What was that for?"

"The kissing?"

"Yeah."

He raises an eyebrow. "Are you saying that I can't kiss the love of my life?"

"No," I say as I crawl toward him, and caress my lips against his. "I'm saying that you're a tease."

He smiles brightly. "No, I'm not."

I straddle him, sliding my hands up his abdomen. "That kiss was very tease-worthy, Trevor George."

"I wasn't trying to tease you," he says sincerely. "I was trying to give myself something good to dream about."

In the shower, water pelts my skin. The hard droplets feel good as they pound into my back, I also feel like a car hood that's been severely dented from the pellets of ice. At first, I turned the water on cold hoping that the icy liquid would extinguish the passionate fire that Trevor had ignited inside of me before I came up here to take this shower. It hasn't really, but I swear I can hear the sizzle as the cold water turns the boiling blood writhing in my veins to frost.

After ten minutes of freezing, I turn the water back to warm, and throw my head back, soothed as the water overheats every part of me. I roll my head back, steam rising off my skin, and drown beneath the shower-head. I hope the hot water burns me from the inside out.

I'm taken aback when the shower curtain's metal rings scrape against the metal rod. My heart races, but I relax when I notice that it's only Trevor. "I thought you were going to sleep," I say, spitting out a mouthful of water.

"I decided that dreaming isn't good enough." He moves closer, entwining his fingers through my wet hair. "Not when I have reality right above me."

He lunges for my mouth, kissing me deeply, tossing water around the inside of my mouth with his tongue. With Trevor, every moment we share together feels like a joyous occasion. I stand there weeping, so full of love and lust and desire that it doesn't even hurt when he hoists me up, snaking my legs around his waist, and slams my back into the tiled wall. I cup the back of his head, gripping onto his matted down strands of gold. I exhale in delight as he moves away from my lips, placing kisses sporadically all over my body. His kisses sear though me, and burn me, but in a very, very good way.

"You're amazing," he says in between kisses. "I love you." His voice is heated and raw and real. It sounds like he's on the precipice of allowing his emotions to completely take over.

"And I love you."

I love him so deeply that sometimes I feel like I'm dreaming. Sometimes I feel like he might be an illusion, and if I put my hands on his skin they might melt right through his shoulder.

Trevor tips my chin up, stares deep into my eyes, and I can't handle not having his lips on mine. I dig my nails into his back, puffing out my bottom lip. "Kiss me." He does. He kisses every inch of the upper half of my body before gently grazing my chin with his teeth. Then he nuzzles his face into the crook of my neck, the stubble on his chin scratching my shoulder.

My shoulder is raw, red, and irritated but I don't care. I'm too far gone in a world of love, bliss, and passion. My emotions are at war with one another. I can't decide if I should laugh, moan in pleasure, or cry. That's what Trevor does to me. He puts my mind in a whirl. He blurs everything. Distorts the lines between what's real and what's not.

I know he's real. I know that for sure when he presses his hips into mine, smothering me with his kisses. But even if he wasn't, I've convinced myself that I'd want to live in a fucked-up fantasy land with the illusion of him. Because a fabricated illusion of Trevor is better than no Trevor at all.

He places his forehead against mine, letting out a long, ragged breath as he thrusts into me. "You set my world on fire." I bite my lip and throw my head back. "I don't know what I'd do without you."

I open my mouth to speak, but he silences me with another gentle caress of his lips against mine. I don't know what I would do without him either.

If I lost Trevor, I know this for sure….

It would kill me.

Chapter
EIGHT

Before

Trevor has been very patient with me over the last three years. Most guys would have given up after six months if their girlfriend wouldn't well, you know, go all the way with them.

Don't get me wrong we've done plenty of *other* things; we've ran around all the bases, we've just never slid into home.

I've never been the type of person to do something just because everybody else is doing it. For the longest time, it felt like everyone that I knew was going all the way. Every time I turned my head, I'd hear another girl whispering about the things they've done while walking down the hallway at school. Even Chloe. She turned in her V card at sixteen.

But I wasn't ready then.

I'm not even sure if I'm ready now.

I like to take my time with things. Projects, relationships, etc. I like to see where things go. In the beginning, I wanted to be sure that I wasn't going to be hit it and quit it material. I wanted to see if Trevor's love for me was as deep as mine was for him. If the roles were reversed, I'd wait for him forever.

I get nervous about big moments like this, and as Trevor walks toward me, his naked silhouette illuminated by the moonlight, I feel like someone collected a jar full of lightning bugs and let them loose inside of me. I know that I should be burning with want for him. I know that I should feel desire pooling between my legs, but I don't. Well, I take that back. Seeing him, like this, all naked, exposed and ready to connect to me both physically and mentally has my heart skipping beats. But there's an even bigger part of me that feels like I'm about to be sick.

I hug my comforter tighter to my naked body while Trevor crawls into bed next to me. He lifts the blanket, sliding underneath, and I can feel his body heat radiating off on him, and onto me. He scoots closer to me. Closer and closer. I feel his bare thigh brush against mine. Little tingles shoot up and down my legs as he positions himself on top of me. I know that I should be looking into his eyes, but I can't bring myself to do it. My eyes wander around the room, ricocheting off lamps and dressers and chairs while a zillion questions hum through my brain.

What if hurts?

What if I get pregnant?

What if I do something wrong?

Gah!

I need to stop. I need to stop overthinking things.

A crinkling wrapper echoes throughout the room, and I know that he's put protection on. Shit. This is really happening. This is really happening. This is really happening. Think fast, Mara. Think fast. Maybe I should fake a leg cramp. Or tell him I think I started my period.

Trevor grazes the tips of his fingers against my cheek, and I exhale. It's crazy to me how one simple gesture could have such a calming effect on me. Inside my head, I'm telling myself to remain calm. I'm telling myself that this, what we have between us, is real. That it's right. He leans down, his bare abdomen pressed against my naked chest. He slips one arm underneath the arch of my back. Our lips are a breath away from each other. Our bodies are close, so close that we could melt together, flesh against flesh and become one.

Seconds pass. Next minutes. We lie in my bed shrouded by darkness with a faint glow of moonlight that's streaming in from my window. Our bare bodies are entangled, limbs everywhere. Trevor's pale blue eyes meet mine in the dark, piercing through my heart, a fire-poker jabbing my hearth. The hearth of my soul.

He wears a gentle expression; a mixture of love, joy, and concern. "We don't have to do this if you don't want to," he says. "If you need more time…."

It's not like I planned to wait for marriage or anything. I planned to wait for love. I planned to wait for the right person, and as my eyes burn into Trevor's, I know that he is the right person. I know that he's the one I've been waiting for. Magically, every shred of doubt, and every nervous feeling I had dwindles away. "No. I want to. I'm ready."

Now I realize that I've never been more certain of anything in my entire life. I love him, and I only have part of him. Part of him isn't good enough. I want all of him.

I sit up slightly, grazing his soft smooth cheek with my fingertips. He leans closer, meeting my lips eagerly with a deep, passionate lip-lock. His kisses are like the ocean, majestic and beautiful and all I want is for him to pull me out farther and farther with the tide.

He kisses my neck, my collarbone, and my jaw before kissing a path up to my ear. "I love you, Mara." he whispers. "You're the only girl I've ever said that to."

I brush my lips against his softly, and reply, "I love you too. You're my one and only."

I'm not an idiot. I know that he has been with other girls. I don't care that someone else had him first. I don't care if I'm a second or third. All that matters is the love we have for one another, and that's what makes this experience feel new. At least to me. Nothing about this first time feels wrong, or off, or gross.

This moment is perfect and beautiful and so right that it's almost frightening. Trevor's fingers glide up my stomach, fanning out across my pale skin before stopping at my chest. I moan, so consumed by my love, my desire, and my passion for him that my legs start trembling.

"Trevor, I…."

He places his lips over mine. "Shhh," he murmurs against my mouth. I open my mouth, inviting his tongue inside for a while, and it dances slowly over top of mine, erotically. "Just let me love you." The words spill into my eager mouth, and I swallow them.

And I do let him love me.

All night long.

Chapter
NINE

After

Trevor gets out of the shower first. He grabs a cream towel from the metal rack next to the sink, and dries off. He tosses me a playful smirk from over his shoulder while handing me the towel. The bathroom is small, and all the walls are white with a white shower curtain to match.

I take the towel, drying off my long, willowy legs first. I stop drying off my legs, focusing on my crooked, bent up toes - remnants of my years as a ballet dancer. It was all I could envision myself doing then. I had my future all mapped out. I would audition for the ABA and dance my life away.

Sometimes life doesn't work out the way you want it to, though. About two weeks before my audition, I shattered two things; my ankle in three places, and my dreams because after I shattered my ankle, the doctor told me that I would never dance en pointe ever again.

Thinking of ballet reminds me of the time that Trevor came to see me as Clara in The Nutcracker. I peek at him from over my shoulder, catching a glimpse of his perfectly toned butt as he walks out of the bathroom. That's the thing about Trevor. He has never once let me down. Anytime he's ever made me a promise, he's kept it. In my opinion, that's the most valuable gift a person could receive. How is possible to trust a person who doesn't stand by their word? It's simple, you can't. You can't trust a person who is a flake.

Trevor waltzes back into the bathroom, a towel wrapped around his waist. I rise to my feet, touching his skin where his hip bones are protruding. He pulls me close to his chest, kissing the top of my head. "I'm going to make some coffee, Mara. You want some?"

I frown up at him, worried. "You need to go back to sleep, Trev. You probably didn't even get an hour."

"How many times do I have to tell you? I'll be fine." He backs away from me. "Do you want coffee or not?"

He's so stubborn and self-sacrificial sometimes. It drives me crazy. But as crazy as he makes me I know him well enough to know how to get what I want. I hang my head low, turning on the fake emotion, sniffling and puffing out my bottom lip. I can cry on command. It's a gift really because it's gotten me things I wanted, and gotten me out of things I didn't want. Tests, speeding tickets, just to name a couple of things.

I raise my head slowly, tears glistening in my eyes. "Please, Trev," I sniffle in between words. "Please."

He gives me a hard look, and steps backwards. "Don't do that," he says pointing his finger. "Mara, I know what you're doing. Don't."

I break out into a full sob. "Trevor, please! I'm so worried about you."

He chuckles nervously, shaking his head. "I know what you're doing, Samara. It's not going to work."

He tells me that every time, but I know him so well. I know that he can't stand to see me cry. He told me once that he loved me so much that when he saw me hurting, it made him hurt. As much as Trevor hates to admit it, he has a sensitive side. He likes to appear to be a badass to everyone else but me. Only I know the real him. The soft, gentle part of him.

I've gotten so good at making my fake sadness look real that sometimes I can't even tell what's real or what's fake anymore. "Trevor!" I cry out as he runs away from me and down the stairs.

"Stop it!" he shouts, his voice ringing out through the whole house.

I chase him, working up even more tears, and heavy breaths. I find him in the kitchen fussing over the French press.

The kitchen is a bit outdated as far as decor goes. The last time it was remodeled must have been the seventies because it's all wood paneling, mustard colored walls and lime green counter tops. The stove is the only thing that looks new. It's stainless steel with a digital clock right in the center of it.

Trevor has his back to me. I slink up to him, wrapping my arms around his waist. "Why do you insist on fighting me?"

He turns, staring into my eyes. I make my lips quiver as tears roll down my cheeks.

Trevor closes his eyes, laughs softly, and shakes his head. "You're good. Too good. You know that?"

I suck back my tears, wiping at the tear-stained presents under my eyes. "I know. I should have considered a career in acting."

Trevor grazes his thumbs over my cheeks, wiping away any remaining wetness. The he brushes his lips against mine. "Promise me you'll wake me in two hours."

I stand on the tips of my toes, kissing his chin with a smile. "I promise." Then again, I could always lose track of time.

He walks to the edge of the kitchen, narrowing his eyes. "Two hours, swear it." I hesitate as a sinister smirk curls on my lips. "I'm serious, Mara. I have to map out a safe route to a new location for us to live in tomorrow. This area is too overrun with the infected."

"Too overrun? No," I say with a hint of sarcasm.

Trevor narrows his eyes. trying not to crack a grin. "Very funny."

On occasion, I've been known not to wake him up when he tells me to. "I swear, Trev."

Trevor walks out of the kitchen, and I listen as the bedroom door slams shut and the coils on the mattress squeak. Relief pulsates in my veins. An overwhelming feeling of comfort settles in the pit of my stomach. Trevor always tries to do too much for me, and I feel elated when I can actually get him to do something for himself.

Seconds later, I linger in the hall across from the bedroom door. The tan colored walls blur in my vision. I close my eyes as Trevor's light snoring throbs in my ears. Then I walk into the kitchen, boil a kettle of water, and make coffee.

After I pour myself a cup of liquid caffeine, I stand at the window, blinds closed, and try to talk myself out of opening them up. But curiosity is driving me batty. I fight against my better judgement, opening them anyway.

The streets are abandoned. Vacant cars line the road. I remember the way the streets used to look when I first moved to this city and I don't I'll ever get used to them looking so dead. Piles of bodies mark every corner, the people in the piles all wearing the same forlorn look. Their eyes are rimmed in red, their faces sunken in, all with bullet holes in their foreheads. That's how you kill the infected. You have to shoot them right between the eyes.

The people here, our neighbors. They are buried amongst the bodies. They were not the living, and they were not the undead. Our infected neighbors contacted the virus, and were cursed to a life of consuming flesh.

A few of the infecteds' carcasses have begun to rot away, their skin ashy and loose. Splotches of infected skin ooze like recently popped blisters. Some even have broken bones protruding through their leather-ish casing. My eyes center on a pile of bodies to my right, only a few feet away from my house. At the bottom of the pile, I see a girl that has to be close to my age. Her vibrant reddish orange hair has been dulled down by death and dirt and she wears the most agonizing look on her face. That look tells me that she didn't deserve to be infected or die the way that she did. So young, and tragic, she barely had a chance to live.

Sometimes I hate the way the Renegades ride in here, massacring the infected to protect what's left of the human population. I know I've said that before. I know that sounds stupid, right? If anything, I should be grateful that they've kept Trevor and I alive to see another day. Maybe I would be if they weren't so relentless and emotionless. Maybe I would like them more if they weren't so cold, with hearts made of ice. Vigilantes on a power trip who think they are doing the government a favor by taking it upon themselves to weed out the infected and bring peace to our world.

Peace. The word should be banned. It's a nasty word that brings false hope. Peace flew away three months ago like a bird flying south for the winter.

When we first moved here, I was sitting on the front porch. I used to go outside sometimes. When we first moved here there weren't too many infected, and we had a little bit more freedom. I saw him, plain as day - the big muscular renegade. I saw him shoot a little girl right in the head. She couldn't have been more than five years old. Sure, she had been infected, but she was just a child. Nobody, infected or not, deserves to die like that.

Backing away from the window, the hurt squirms inside of me like earthworms breaking through the surface of the wet ground after an intense round of rain. Tears swell in my eyes, and I swallow a lump in my throat as I walk to the opposite side of the room. I tell myself that I won't look outside again until they find a way to cure all of the infected people in the world.

And who knows when that will be.

Chapter
TEN

Before

It's dark in my bedroom. I lie in my bed with Trevor, enveloped in his arms, my cheek against his bare chest.

Moonlight gleams in from the windows, casting shadows against the pale pink walls. It's quiet, but Trevor's light breathing swells in my ears. "Trev," I say softly, staring up at him. His eyes are slit open the tiniest bit. As the moonlight dances over his face, I can make out a hint of sapphire beneath his dark lashes. "Are you awake?"

"Hmm," he moans. "Yeah, kind of." I lift my head off of his chest, and reposition my pillow underneath my head. Trevor rolls over, facing me, tucking a strand of my hair behind my ear. "What is it, baby?"

"For some reason, I can't sleep," I let out in a breath. I play with the drawstrings on his pants. "I don't know why."

He reaches out, slipping his hand over the dip in my waist, pulling me closer. We entwine our legs together, and with a soft grazing touch he runs his fingers through my hair. "Is something bothering you?" His lips brush against mine, and I taste his orange-mint flavored tooth paste.

He keeps his eyes on me, but I drop my head, fidgeting with my fingers. "Not really." Sometimes I get like this. Restless. Nothing is really bothering me, but I'm thinking about random things like leaving for college in four weeks. My parents are two rooms over, and I'm wondering why they agreed to letting Trevor spend the night. They are pretty strict when it comes to me being alone with Trevor. In the past, we've always had to sneak around or wait until they went out of town just to get any alone time together.

Trevor cuts into the silence when he says, "Do you want to know a secret?"

"A secret?" I prop myself up on my elbow, and frown. "We don't have any secrets."

"I have one," he says in a low voice that sends a chill throughout my entire body.

I sit all the way up, balling my fists at my sides. "I'm not sure if I want to hear this." I clench my jaw, looking away from him. "Did you—did you," I stutter. "Did you cheat on me?" What else could he be keeping from me? I'm terrified to hear what his answer might be because I know that if he cheated our relationship would be over, and I'd never be able to get over it.

He sits up and grips my arm and my head snaps toward him. "Cheat on you?" His voice raises an octave. "Do you honestly think I'd do that?"

My eyes scan him briefly, taking in the hurt expression on his gorgeous face. "Well Trevor, when you spring something like this on me what do you expect me to think?" I scoot closer to him. "I thought we had an open and honest relationship. I thought we told each other everything."

"I'm ashamed of it. I thought that you'd dump me if you found out, and I couldn't handle it if I lost you, Mara," he says, his voice layered thick with emotion.

"Trevor." I take both of his hands in mine, massaging his thumbs with mine, "don't you know that nothing you could have done would have kept me away? I love you too much."

"Maybe not now, but in the beginning, it might have."

"No." I shake my head, and brush the back of my hand against his cheek. "Never."

"Those rumors about me being in juvie are true."

He lifts his head slightly, his eyes wary, waiting for my reaction. I start laughing. "Is that all?"

He frowns. "Is that all?" he scoffs. "Is that all? How can you think that's funny?"

"So you made a few mistakes in your past and got in trouble for them. You're obviously not the same person. I don't understand why you made such a big deal out of telling me that. I still love you, reckless past and all."

I lean down to kiss his forehead and he pulls away from me, running his hand through his hair with a grunt. "I didn't make a mistake. I did it on purpose."

"Well, what did you do then?"

"I beat up some guy so bad he was hospitalized."

"Why?" My Trevor is the kindest, gentlest, and most loyal person I know. He's never once displayed any kind of aggression.

"He tried to rape my sister. She brought him home a few times, and I never liked him, you know? He had this slimy way about him. He was always grabbing at her in a dirty way. But I just figure that some guys are like that." He's right. Not all men are like that, but there are definitely some that are. "Anyway, you know Claire, she's older and likes to play the I'm-independent-and-I-can-take-care-of-myself game." I've only met Claire a few times. She's been away at college for most of our relationship. But from what I know of her, she is so sweet and down to earth. And she definitely gave off a headstrong kind of vibe. The same with his mother. She'd give you the shirt off her back if you needed it. His father has pretty much been out of the picture since he was born. One of those types that fathered a child, but didn't want the responsibility of being a parent.

"One time I told her I didn't like the way he touched her, and do you know what she said?"

What did she say?"

"She told me to butt out, and mind my own business. So I did. I let her do her thing until my mom got a call late one night. Claire had gone with that piece of shit to a frat party. I could hear her on the other end of the phone shrieking and screaming hysterically. At that moment, I knew. She didn't even need to tell me. I knew that that piece of shit had done something to her. After that, Mom grabbed her keys, went and picked her up and took her to the police station to fill out a report. And do you know what the cops did?"

I shake my head.

"Nothing," he says in a low chilling voice. "They did nothing. There were no other witnesses because the kid locked the door to the room and Claire had to climb down the garden trellis to escape. He hit her too. When she came home, her entire face was bruised up like a rotten apple."

"Oh my God."

"He denied it, of course. He denied it because that's what true genuine pieces of shit do."

"Trevor," I gasp as tears flood my eyes. "Poor Claire." My heart breaks when I think of what she had to go through.

"What was the worst was listening to her cry herself to sleep every night for a week." He looks at me sincerely. "You know how much I love my mom and sister. You know how much family means to me."

I nod. That's usually the only time he ever blows me off is if he's helping one them with something. "I do." A tear drips down my chin, and Trevor wipes it away.

"Two weeks later, Claire started therapy. She seemed to be doing better. One day she came home, and I was in the kitchen making a bowl of cereal. She walked over to me, grabbed me by the arm, and hugged me, hard. Seconds later her whole body began shaking and she cried, 'I should have listened to you, Trevor. I should have listened to you.'

"It was during that moment that I snapped. Went crazy. Completely lost it. I grabbed a baseball bat from the garage, found out where the kid lived, and went to his house. You should have seen the smug look on that bastard's face when he answered the door and saw me there. A second later, I pulled out the bat. Everything went black after that. But I do know that he wound up in the hospital for a while, and I wound up in juvie for three months. After I got out, Mom moved us, and I started a new life."

After listening to his confession, I sit across from him still holding his hand. I'm unable to say anything, and I'm not sure why. I can't decide if I'm more stunned that the Trevor I know and love has a dark side that I've never seen or more hurt for him and his family, knowing what they had to go through to get over something like that.

Trevor cuts into the quiet, and says, "Say something."

I don't answer. I don't know what to say.

Trevor pulls his hands out of my grasp, turning a cheek to me. "Now you hate me, don't you?"

I grip his wrist, pulling him toward me. "Why would you think that?" I inhale deeply, and exhale slowly. "How many times do I have to tell you, I love you? I will never hate you. I will never think any less of you." What he did wasn't necessarily the best thing for him to do, but I imagine if I had siblings and someone had wronged one of them that I'd want to do the same thing.

I pull his head to my chest, lying back on the bed. "You should hate me, Mara. You should be afraid of me."

"You don't scare me one bit, Trevor David George." I kiss every inch of his face before planting a long, lingering kiss on his lips.

He pulls out of the kiss, looking up at me, studying my expression. "But you should be."

"Should be, what?"

"Afraid."

I tsk. "Why do you think I should be afraid?"

He swallows hard, and I can feel his jaw tighten beneath my fingertips. "Because if anyone ever did anything like that to you, I wouldn't stop with hospitalizing them. I'd fucking kill them."

Chapter
ELEVEN

After

Trevor has only been sleeping for an hour, so I do mundane things to pass the time before I have to go wake him. I count the boxes of ammo we have stored away in our weapons closet. I check the pantry for any remaining canned goods that we'll need to pack when we leave tomorrow morning. Then I grab all the duffels from the coat closet, and set them on the floor in the kitchen.

I wait until about fifteen minutes before I'm supposed to wake him, and I go into the bedroom, sitting down across from him. He's shirtless, abs taut, his arms stretched above his head, twisted behind his shimmering gold locks. I can't do anything but stare because even in his contorted wild haze of slumber he's the most beautiful man I've ever seen.

My fingers tremble as I reach out to touch him. I want his touch. I need his touch. I swear that I can feel it my bones. When his fingertips glide against mine, the feel of them shocks me, burns me, and fills me up with delight. I pull my hand back, deciding against touching him so that I can allow him every precious minute of sleep he can get.

Minutes pass. I lie next to Trevor, my eyes planted on the ceiling with uncertainty swimming in my gut. I'm worried about tomorrow. I don't know how everything is going to go down, and it's the not knowing that scares me the most.

Trevor moans, curling his long arm around my shoulder. He squeezes tightly while he stretches and yawns. "Please don't tell me that you let me sleep more than two hours."

My eyes center on the white clock hanging above the bedroom door. Not that I'd call it a bedroom. It's a few mahogany dressers, and a flimsy mattress on the floor. There's a thick layer of gray dust frosting the front of the clock, but I can still make out the black hands. "Nope. It's been two hours exactly."

Trevor unlaces his arm from my shoulder, sitting up. "Did you make coffee?"

"Yeah, but it's probably gross by now. I'll make more."

Trevor waves me off. "Don't worry about it. I'll just drink it cold."

"It's not a big deal. I can make more."

"I have a busy day. Don't worry about it."

He stands, throwing his arms up in a stretch, and I admire the indents in his back, right above his butt. The perfect resting spot for my hands. I remember the first time we ever, well, you know, and a smug grin unfurls on my lips.

He glances over his shoulder, beaming at me. "What are you so happy about?"

I play it off coyly. "Oh, nothing." And then I fall back onto the bed with a sigh.

Trevor shakes his head with a hungry look in his eye. Then he jumps on top of me. We laugh in unison as his fingers crawl up my arm before he traces my jawline with his forefinger. "No, seriously," he says. "What were you thinking about?" His lips are an inch away from my face, and all I can think about is how badly I want them on mine. I've become a junkie, so eager to get high off him. The only thing I can think about is how badly I want the needle to puncture my skin.

You...

You are my drug.

I want you.

I need you.

Please, please, please.

It's amazing how he can set my organs on fire with one, gentle caress of his fingertips. It's amazing how when I'm near him I start to forget about everything. The outbreak. The loss of friends, family, and neighbors. It's amazing how time seems to stand still whenever he's around.

Sometimes my love for him smothers every other emotion inside of me. Sometimes I have to remind myself that I'm supposed to feel other things like happiness, depression, and grief. I'm crackling, sizzling, and fizzing before I go kaboom. "I thought you were too busy today. You don't have time to talk about what I'm thinking about."

He squints his eyes, leaning in closer to my face. "I'll make time."

"Oh," I say with a laugh. "So now you'll make time?"

His lips brush against my ear, and a delightful flutter full of fire and seduction swirls around my stomach. Twenty cocoons have just hatched inside of me, and there are butterflies flitting around flapping their wings. They are thankful to be free of their skin casing. They are thankful they aren't larva anymore.

Trevor pecks my lips, gliding his fingers down my breastbone, and stops placing his palm flat on my stomach. "Tell me." There's an urgency in his voice, a heated look in his eyes.

"I was just regaling in past moments." I think of the shower earlier, and a soft blush creeps up my neck, taking up residence in my cheeks.

He crooks me a beautiful and sinister smile. I love it when he smiles. His whole face lights up. He's icicle lights hanging above the garage during Christmas. He's twinkling. "Ohhhh." He bites his bottom lip, staring at me teasingly. "Well then," he trails off. "Let me refresh your memory."

Trevor stands in the kitchen with his hands on his hips in front of a map he'd drawn out on the green wall with a charcoal-like crayon. I pour him a cup of fresh coffee, black just like he likes it, then slip my arms through the keyhole slots of his arms, and squeeze him. "Thanks, love." He takes the cup from my right hand, bringing it to his lips.

He takes a giant gulp from the mug and we both stare at the map. I find myself giggling. The smudges of back x's, rectangles, triangles, and various lines reminds me of something juvenile. A toddler could have done a better job of drawing this map. "Well," I lament. "Now we know that art is not a strong point of yours."

Trevor tosses me a smirk from over his shoulder. "Hey," he holds his hands up, "I never said it was."

I unlace my arms from around his waist, stepping to the side, moving closer. "What are the x's for?" I assume they stand for the infected, but as I gape at the chicken scratch further, it's hard to tell.

Trevor sets his mug down on the edge of the counter. "The infected." And I assumed right. He takes a step forward, and points at the map. "See the places where the x's are in clusters?"

I nod, and lean against the counter.

"Those are the areas that are overrun with the infected." I know he knows his stuff because he's the one that's always going out there. He's the one that really gets to see the world for what it has become, a pile of rubble festering with disease, and decay. He glances at me then back at the makeshift map. "The triangle down here," he points to a smudged triangle in the far-right hand corner of the map, "this is us. And the parallel lines just below the triangle is the safe zone."

I focus on the triangle, pointing. "So this is us?" He nods. "And the parallel lines are the safe zones." His chicken scratch is hard to understand.

Trevor lets out a frustrated sigh. "Yes. For the love of Christ, we've already gone over this." He gestures to the map. "The parallel lines are areas that haven't been overrun...yet."

The smudged triangle resembling us burns into my eyes and I can't seem to look at any other spot on the map. Mainly because the parallel lines are below us. "So we're not safe at all?" I know the question seems silly, but I need to hear the answer from him. The truth is that no one is safe.

"Correct." Trevor nods to the triangle on the opposite side of the map. "The triangle on the other side is our new place. It's a solid location, there are hardly any infected, and the Renegade headquarters are right next door."

I see where he's going with this and I don't want any part of it. "I'm not going." I don't even like looking at the Renegades when they ride in here on their motorcycles leaving trails of blood in their wake, let alone living with them. I bet they want him to join up too. I won't have it.

Trevor rolls his eyes. "Mara be reasonable."

"You know how I feel about them."

"Believe me, love, I know. But we have to consider what is going to be best for us. Especially when it comes to survival. Do you know that they've built an electric fence to keep the infected out? They just finished it. I've seen it."

I sigh, defeated. The truth is, I want to survive. I want to live to see the future. I want to see the look on my children's faces. I guess that living with people I don't like is just something that I'm going to have to live with. "So, when do we leave?"

"First thing in the morning. We'll pack only what we need, and move out on foot at dawn."

I raise an eyebrow. "On foot?" I think of the infected that lurk in dark places just waiting. Watching. Starving. Hoping that some mindless, fleshy human will come along and ring their dinner bell.

He picks up his cup of coffee, takes, a swig, sets it down, and crosses his arms. "I'll push my bike, and you can carry the luggage."

"I don't think that's very smart. I think we'd have a better chance if we rode on the bike."

"We can't ride the bike." He throws his arms up in the air. "It's only about an hour walk. Two tops."

The idea of walking several miles on foot in an area that's been overrun with the infected doesn't feel right. in fact, the thought of it makes my skin crawl. "What if we have a run in with one of the infected? Why can't we just ride your bike over there?"

"Mara, stop being so dense. You know the infected are attracted to noise. We have to be as quiet as possible and my bike will be too loud."

"But you take your bike out all the time!" I've seen him ride off on plenty of occasions. His rude comment about me being dense pisses me off. "And I am not dense, Trevor," I snap, and toss him a scowl. "I know they're attracted to noise, but the bike is faster and the infected won't be able to keep up."

"Those are always quick trips. Places that are seconds away. We can't take the bike out over a long haul; it will attract every infected person from here to Asia."

I'll admit that I do have absent-minded moments, but that's because Trevor tries to do everything on his own, and never lets me help. "And I wouldn't make any comments about it if you stopped trying to do everything on your own and actually let me help." He's really irritating my soul right now.

Trevor touches my arm, and for the first time ever, I don't want his hands on me. I twist away from him, looking in the opposite direction. "Mara, I'm sorry," he apologizes. "You're right. You should know what it's like out there. You should see it so that you can be prepared. I just thought it would be best because I know how frightened you are of the infected in general. I was trying to protect you."

"Well maybe you shouldn't. Maybe you should teach me how to protect myself." I need to learn. What if it came down to a situation where he wasn't there to protect me? What then?

He narrows his eyes, and a hard look washes over his face. "Maybe I will."

"Good," I snap.

"Good!" he scoffs and walks out of the room. "You have issues, you know that?"

I chase after him. "What's that supposed to mean?" I wave my finger at him as I come up behind him.

He turns a corner, storming up the steps as I follow close behind. "It means you're stubborn and have some sort of sadistic death wish."

No, I don't. I'm just completely co-dependent, and for once would like to feel like I've done something. For once I would like to feel like I can be useful. "*You* have a problem, you know that!"

"And what exactly is that?" He makes quotation marks with his fingers. "Come on. Fill me in, Samara. I'd love to know what kind of problem you think I have."

"Fine!" I snap, balling up my fists, and slamming them at my sides. "It's like you want to keep me in this little bubble. You want me to keep on living in this deluded fantasy that everything is fine even though it isn't so that I'll have to depend on you for everything. Trevor, I'm sick of it! I'm sick of you thinking that I'm the naive fourteen-year-old who was so nervous that she couldn't even speak to you. I'm getting sick of you treating me like I won't be of any help to you out there when I know I will be." Trevor grimaces, grits his teeth then disappears into an empty bedroom. "Where are you going? I'm talking to you!"

I keep my back against the wall on the staircase, listening to pings as Trevor rummages through our weapons closet. He emerges from the bedroom, shoving a gun in his pants. I don't get a clear look at the weapon. I know it's a gun, but all I can see is something long, cylindrical and black on the end of it. He grabs me by the arm, and pulls me down the stairs. He's angry, breathing heavily, and tightening his grip on my arm. "Where are we going?"

"You want to get up close, and personal with the infected, well, I aim to please you, Samara Moore."

"I've been up close and personal with the infected, Trevor. What in the hell is this about?"

85

"Not like this, you haven't."

He yanks open the front door with force, and we walk out onto the rickety wooden porch. It's been a while since I've been out here. I almost forgot what the porch looked like. The wooden planks are rotting and falling apart in places, and the muted pewter paint is almost chipped all the way off. Rusted metal rungs hang on the ceiling, a reminder that a porch swing used to dangle there. I glare at him warily, mixed with fear and rage. I fold my arms across my chest and scowl. "Well?"

"Well." Trevor slits his eyes and cocks his head to the side. "Look for yourself."

I almost don't want to. There's a cowardly part of me that wants to run back into the house, and tell Trevor that he was right. That the world is too harsh for me to face. That I'll just go on forever being completely co-dependent on him. I'll let him protect me, being his good obedient lover, doing whatever he tells me to. But the stubbornness in me overrides the cowardice so I snap my head to the right defiantly staring out into the vacant streets. Besides, if I admit he's right, I know him, he'll gloat. And then I'll have to hear about this moment for the rest of our time together. Trevor's gloating gets old really fast.

I focus on the empty streets, decorated with trash and bodies. It reminds me of a dilapidated landfill. The buildings that line the streets are dark, dirty, and abandoned. They look dead, like the bodies lining the streets. I can see holes in the windows from rocks being tossed at them. There's no sound—no sound of the suburban life whatsoever. The only thing I hear is the raspy breath exiting my throat. I wait for something to happen.

Anything really, but nothing does. It's like we live in a ghost town, and I can't understand why Trevor wants to keep me locked up in the house. I turn toward him, rolling my eyes. "Ohhh, I'm terrified," I say sarcastically. "There aren't even any infected here."

It's not like I haven't seen them from the window or heard them pounding into our door at night. I don't get it. What did they do? Did they decide that maybe they needed a vacation?

An Alaskan Cruise, perhaps?

Trevor gives me a hard look. "Just wait."

"For what?"

"Shhhh."

I wait. For seconds. Minutes. I'm not really sure how much time passes, but then I hear it—soft scraping like shoes scuffing against the blacktop. Out of the corner of my eye I see one of the infected limping across the pavement. A man. A man so thin I can see his cheekbones. He opens his mouth and moans; his teeth are cracked and chipped off. His skin dangles like loose clothing and jiggles as his cries intensify. He has me and Trevor in his sights and he picks up his pace, breaking out into a half-limp half-jog. He growls fiercely, white saliva dripping from his jaw like a dog with rabies. There is dried blood crusted in the corners of his mouth, a remnant of his last meal.

I can't move. It's like my feet are stuck in wet concrete. It doesn't matter how many times I try to move, I can't and Trevor waits patiently behind me. I glimpse at him from over my shoulder, the fear in my eyes meeting his shimmering set of sapphires. "Trevor," my vocal chords quiver. The sour taste of panic gathers in my throat.

Why isn't he doing anything? Why hasn't he whipped out the gun, and shot this man already? Because he's Trevor and he's trying to prove a point.

Plunk, plunk, plunk. I listen to the sound of the man's slow steps as he climbs the wooden stairs. I'm so consumed with fear and panic and absolute horror that I swear that I can almost taste the rotted flesh as the man howls, breathing into my face. That's when Trevor moves behind me.

And he's quick.

His arm flies out across my chest, shoving me behind him. I stumble and fall, scraping my hands against the wood. I'm certain the infected man can smell the crimson drops of blood dripping from my hands. I close my eyes, afraid to open them. I'm so afraid yet at the same time I'm angry. I'm angry that I was so defenseless and that Trevor had to come to my rescue.

There's a scuffle going on in front of me, and I cry, "Trevor!"

All of a sudden there's no movement, and I'm stunned into silence when I hear the sound of a body dropping against the hollowed out wooden planks.

Chapter TWELVE

Before

Trevor paces in front of me and my eyes follow him. "I can't believe you want to fight about this right now!" he growls.

I stand across from him in my driveway, my hands on my hips. "I'm not trying to fight with you, Trev, I'm trying to talk to you rationally," I shoot back.

This whole argument started because I'm leaving for college in two weeks, and I want him to come with me. "You should have told me this months ago, Mara, not weeks ago!"

I grit my teeth. "I did tell you months ago, but you weren't listening to me!" I swear, sometimes I think he's deaf. I could tell him the same thing like ten times in a row and on the eleventh time he'd still ask me what I said. I throw my hands in the air in frustration. "God, you're impossible sometimes, you know that?"

His eyes widen, and he points to his chest. "I'm impossible?" He shakes his head letting out a laugh laced with a little bit of craziness. "Woman, you coined the term impossible."

"I did not!" I stomp my foot into the cement. "What? Am I so wrong for wanting you to be with me? Is it wrong of me to ask for a life with you?"

"You know that I've been saving up since I was sixteen so that I could open up my own mechanic shop. It's like you expect me to give up everything I've worked so hard for just like that."

"But you can fix cars anywhere," I insist.

It's not that I don't want him to be able to have his dreams, I do. It's just that he hasn't even thought of where he's going to put his mechanic shop yet. He could put it anywhere. If he could start one up here, then he could definitely start one up in the city. On top of that, I can't help how deep my love runs for him. Even after three years. I can't help that I want to spend every second with him.

"You're just mad because you broke your ankle and shattered your dreams, and it will make you feel better if you ruin mine as well," he sneers.

Now, he's really done it. "How fucking dare you?" I think about slapping him, but I refrain. Instead my eyes go wide shimmering with wetness, and I clutch my heart. "How can you say that?" My lips quivers, and I swallow hard. "How could you ever think that of me?"

Trevor exhales and regret crosses over his features. I scowl, holding back tears, and look away from him, folding my arms across my chest. On top of my anger, I'm in complete and total shock. I can't believe he just went there. That blow was so low. Untrue and low.

He walks over to me, places two fingers under my chin, and I jerk my head away. "Mara, look at me." His warm breath wafts over my face, and I inhale the smell of mint. "I'm sorry, I shouldn't have said that."

I face him, anger blazing in my eyes, and say coldly, "No you shouldn't have." I would have never said anything like that to him. He lifts a hand to my cheek. I slap it away. "Did you ever think that maybe I wanted you to come with me because I loved you that much? Did you ever think that I wanted you to come with me because for me the sun sets and rises with you? I love you so much that sometimes I feel like it's suffocating me." I take a deep breath, close my eyes, and pinch the bridge of my nose. "I...I...I" I struggle to find words.

I've heard the phrase if you love something set it free, if it comes back it's meant to be. All I want if for Trevor to be happy, and if he'll be happy here fixing cars then so be it. It's time for me to grow up and be an adult about things, even though there's a dull throbbing ache in my side, pumping pain throughout my entire body like an air ventilation system when I contemplate what I'm about to do. "We might as well stop this, Trevor," I say, the emotion cracking in my voice. "We might as well just end this now."

He staggers backwards, a flash of pain sparking in his beautiful blue eyes. He shakes his head. "You don't mean that, Mara."

Of course I didn't mean it. The words tasted rancid, like bile, when I spit them out, but I've seen plenty of couples go through the same thing. They always tried in the beginning—you know with the whole long-distance thing—and it never ended up working out. "I'm just trying to be realistic, Trev." We've lived in our own little bubble for the last three years and now it's time to grow up and face the real world. "I just think it will be harder on us if we try and it fails," I choke out, holding back the sob that's stuck in my throat.

It kills me that I'm lying to him, but I know that I have to. The hardship of a long-distance relationship isn't the only reason that I'm trying to push him away. Taking a step closer to him, I gaze lovingly into his pools of blue. I admire his angular jawline. He's such a beautiful, selfless, amazing man. I would hate to be the reason he gave up everything he's worked so hard for. Deep down inside I know that if I did hold him back from doing what he really wanted, he'd end up resenting me, and that's something I couldn't live with.

"So give up before we even start," he scoffs, and turns walking toward his bike.

"Hey." I yank on his arm, but he shoves me off. "Hey!"

He spins around, but won't look me in the eye. "What?" He's all over the place; kicking a rock on the ground, flicking a piece of fuzz off the sleeve of his leather jacket. He is doing everything he can to avoid looking at me.

"You think I want this? You know how you make me feel. You're the only guy I've ever loved."

"I'm the only guy you've ever dated."

"So?" I fold my arms across my chest, and jut out my hip. "What does that have to do with any of this?"

Trevor closes his eyes. letting out a long, winded sigh. It's like he's psyching himself up for something really big. Then he stuffs his fists into his pockets of his faded, worn jeans. "Maybe you're right then."

"Wait…what?"

"Maybe we should end things now."

My heart aches—no—throbs. I feel like my left ventricle has just collapsed. I know I said the same exact thing minutes earlier, but it sounded worse coming from him. Not only that, but when I said the words I didn't really mean them. I mean it was just a fight, right? In two minutes we'll go back to being the loving couple we've always been. If I had to let him go in the future, I'd worry about it in the future, not now. More than that, the finality in his voice made the words leaving his lips sound like a death sentence, and I fight off all the emotion inside of me that's rising to the surface.

I lower my head. This is all my fault. I blink back more tears, lifting my head. I started this, and I don't want to go on hysterics in front of him, but I'm having a hard time keeping my composure.

Trevor walks toward me, takes my face in his hands, and examines my features thoughtfully. His thumbs gently massage my cheekbones. I exhale as the tingle from his touch spreads throughout my entire body. His eyes sear into mine, moving back and forth like a human lie detector. His blue eyes are probing my brown ones. They're searching my soul for the truth. Then he leans in, his lips almost touching mine and says, "I'll always love you, Mara. Good luck with your life." A second later, he places a short, painful kiss on my cheek. He turns his back to me, and walks to his bike.

No. Come back. I'm thinking the words, but I can't speak them. I'm moving my mouth, but nothing is coming out. Trevor please. Please stay. Go with me. Love me.

The only body language I can muster up is staring. I stare at his jaw remembering the way his chiseled muscles in jaw flexed when he kissed me. I stare at the back of his leather jacket remembering every summer ride, every kiss, and every explicit moment that happened on that bike.

And lastly, I stare at the Ducati, the silver paint, gleaming in the sunlight, as it speeds down the driveway, and Trevor speeds out of my life forever.

Chapter THIRTEEN

After

"I don't know why you had to do that," I tell Trevor as he cleans the cuts on my hands.

I think about what happened earlier. About the fight that led to all of this.

Trevor and I rarely fight. Sure, we bicker about stupid stuff like who left the milk out or because one of us insists on doing something so the other won't have to, but other than that, we have a smooth and loving relationship. I watched a few people I knew in high school go through break ups and make ups repeatedly. In fact, it happened so much it made my head spin.

Trevor and I only broke up once. Well, if you even count twenty-one days as a breakup.

At the end of June, I moved to Boston for college. I moved early so that I could get settled into my apartment, and get to know the city a little bit. I actually dumped him because I convinced myself that a long-distance relationship wasn't going to work.

Three weeks later, at my apartment in Boston, my doorbell rang, and I opened the door to see Trevor, one shoulder dipped in propped up against the doorframe with a cocky smile curled on his lips. "So," he said, straightening himself out. "I was thinking that this break up thing kind of sucks."

I didn't give him the opportunity to say anything else. I latched on his neck and smashed my lips into his. Never again, never again, never again, bounced around inside of my brain like a drumbeat.

Never again would I even think of being apart from him. Never again would I say the words, "Maybe we should end this." The three weeks I spent apart from him devastated me. I became this void—this shell of a human being. There was a severe pain in my heart, a numbness in my gut. Mostly I found no joy in anything that existed. I couldn't eat. I couldn't sleep. I was a walking nightmare with an empty soul, and an emotionless expression.

And I never wanted to feel that way ever again.

I belong with Trevor. I belong in his arms. I belong in his heart. There isn't a minute that passes by that I don't think about him. There isn't a minute that goes by where my heart doesn't race the second I see him. He is my forever.

Trevor cuts into my thoughts when he replies with, "Do what?" He pours some peroxide into my open wounds.

"Don't play dumb," I snap. "I know you know what I'm talking about, Trevor David."

"Oh no," he says with a chuckle. "She's using the middle name. I must be in trouble."

The peroxide fizzles out of the cuts disinfecting them. The white bubbling liquid reminds me of the saliva dripping from that infected man's mouth. I shudder, and wince as the liquid works its way through my skin. Seconds later, I feel like both of my hands are on fire. "Ouch! Trevor!" I try to pull my hands away, but Trevor tightens his grip. "That hurts!"

He flashes me a brilliant smile while placing a bandage on each of my hands. "Quit whining, you big baby."

"Stop it," I laugh, feeling suddenly at ease. The laughter dies down when I think about what just happened on the porch. "Seriously, Trev. Why did you wait until last minute to shoot that infected man?"

"I wanted you to experience the severity of what's going on out there." He rolls his eyes upward while he screws the lid onto the peroxide. "You said that you wanted to help. You said that I made you live in a bubble. Well love, you were just outside of that bubble. I know you've seen a few things go down from the window and when we fled, but that's nothing compared to what goes on out in the world every day. You think one infected person is bad?" Trevor shakes his head then looks deeply into my eyes. "Try being in the middle of a group of them. They keep coming at you, and coming at you. It's like they won't rest until they've picked your bones clean."

A wave of nausea circles through my stomach when I think about the words, picked your bones clean. I try my best to erase them from my mind, but I'm afraid they will be permanently embedded there. "I don't care, Trevor. From now on, if you go, I go. I can't bear the thought of you being out there alone, fighting them off. What if you're bitten? What if somehow you become infected? I'll tell you this, if anything ever happened to you, I don't know if I would be able to handle it."

"I'll tell you what I'd want you to do if I ever became infected…"

"I want you to teach me how to defend myself. I want to know how to fire a gun," I say cutting him off. He's already told me what he'd want me to do if he ever became infected.

Trevor gets up and walks across the kitchen, gazing out the window. "Maybe that isn't such a bad idea after all."

My eyes widen with excitement. "Really?" I know he kind of said that he was going to teach me how to defend myself, but that doesn't necessarily mean he will. It's true that he's never broken a promise that he's made me, but over the last four years, I've come to know that the love of my life truly enjoys being the alpha male type. For some reason, he thrives on protecting me. Not that I'm complaining, I love that protective part of him. I just don't want to always feel like I'm sitting there waiting for him to come to my rescue. Sometimes I'd like to be able to try and save myself before he swoops in to save the day.

INFECT ME

Trevor makes his 'I'm thinking' face where he slits his eyes, scrunches his eyebrows together, and wrinkles his nose. "Yes, really."

I replay the moment on the porch where I was reacting like a moron before I heard the body slump against the wood. For a second, my eyes were still closed, and I thought that something might have happened to Trevor because I didn't hear a blast from the gun. "Why didn't the gun make a noise?"

Trevor takes off his thinking helmet, facing me. "What?"

"I didn't hear a blast when you fired the gun." I don't know too much about guns. I know how many we have, and I know which bullet matches each type of gun that Trevor has collected on his various raids, but other than that, I need to be filled in.

"That's because there is a silencer on it. And thank God for that. A loud blast coming from a gun would attract every infected person from here to Delaware. It's like those fuckers have radars implanted in their ears so they can hear that shit."

"How many guns do we have that have silencers on them?" It's obvious that I know where we keep the weapons, and I have access to them, but I've never had to use one before.

He crooks me a devilish grin. "Wouldn't you like to know?"

This is a serious conversation. I'm not in the mood to play games or be toyed with. "Seriously, how many?"

Trevor slits his eyes, staring me. I can tell he senses the seriousness in my tone. The smile fades from his lips. "Two out of the four have silencers on them."

"Great," I announce as a smile pulls on my lips. "One for you. One for me."

He eyes me oddly, tightening his lips. "Hmm," he says. I can tell by his mannerisms that me toting a weapon and going out on supply runs with him is going to be a major adjustment.

When we first started dating, one thing that I loved – that I still love – about Trevor is that he's old fashioned. He was always opening doors for me, pulling out chairs for me when we went to eat somewhere, and he always walked me to my front door at the end of our dates.

One of the main reasons why I think Trevor acts like my protector is because his father abandoned him when he was just a baby, and it was just him, his mom, and his sister when he was growing up.

On our fourth date, he mentioned something to me that his mom said to him. "Women deserve to be treated with respect, Trevor David. We can love fiercely, passionately, and wholeheartedly, but not if we're treated like a man's flavor of the week. You got that, son?"

"And what about ammo?" I ask him.

"What about it?"

"I just counted the boxes while you were sleeping."

Trevor reaches over, setting the peroxide down on the counter. "Remind me of how many boxes we have."

"Six," I tell him. "Do you think that's enough to last us for a while?"

"I'd say that's going to last us two to three weeks."

"What's going to happen when we run out?"

Trevor stares off, lost in a world of oblivion. Out of all the years we've been together, it's a world I've never seen him in.

He's always so sure of himself. He's always got a plan. And it's weird to see the expression on his face that tells me his mind has gone blank. "Honestly, Mara, I don't know."

I look down at the square band aid on my right palm, and brush my forefinger against it. The texture of it reminds me of Trevor. Rough on the outside, soft on the inside. Like an Oreo cookie. "Trevor," I say, looking at him earnestly.

"Yes, Mara."

"How long do you think we'll survive like this?"

Trevor opens a drawer, and places the first aid supplies inside. Then he closes the drawer, but keeps his eyes on the metal handle. "In a world like this, God only knows."

The following morning, I help Trevor pack our belongings. "Only pack the absolute necessities," he tells me as he removes all of the ammunition from our weapons and packs it in a duffle bag beneath a mountain of clothes. He pats down the overflowing articles of clothing, zips up the bag, and tosses it onto the floor. The he walks over to me, glancing into my open duffle. "How's it coming, love?"

"Good," I say as he kisses my temple. He walks to the other side of the room, picking up another empty bag from the floor. He begins filling it with canned goods.

I don't want him to know or see what I've been packing. Yes, I've packed a few necessities, like underwear and bandages and rubbing alcohol, but I've also been packing other things—

mementos. The things that I've kept throughout our relationship that remind me of him. Of us. A set of movie stubs from the first film that we ever saw together. Framed photos. A dried up rose boutonniere that Trevor wore on his tuxedo to our first dance. Lord Byron's 'She Walks in Beauty,' a poem he ripped out of a library book, and gave to me on our six-month anniversary. And lastly, a frayed tattered piece of the first leather jacket I ever saw him in.

These items are not necessities, but they are too precious to me to part with. And I know exactly what Trevor would say if he saw them. He'd tell me that while the thought of keeping them is sweet, we need to be realistic and make room in the duffle for more important things like extra clothes and extra canned goods. But I can't. I can't part with them, and I won't let him make me.

Don't get me wrong, I'm sure the memories of our time together are precious to Trevor too, but out of the two of us he's the more practical one. He thinks about survival first and foremost while I thrive on living in the past. We had such a beautiful past after all. Sometimes he'll look at me and say, "The past is the past, Mara. I don't know why you insist on living there."

I usually reply with, "Because I like it there."

What I can't tell him, what I won't tell him, what I'll never tell him is that the only beauty left in my life is in my memories. When I think of my future, I'm always on edge, always anxious, always scared. The future is grim and uncertain and full of infected people who only have worms for brains and flesh on their minds. When I think of our future, as much as I hate to admit it, I don't know if we'll have one.

I never used to be a cynic. But since the outbreak, I've seen things I wish I hadn't seen. I watched people change before my eyes, I've witnessed countless murders. I watched an infected man bite into one of my neighbor's arms, devouring it like it was a chicken wing, and he wouldn't be satisfied until he could use the bones to pick his teeth. At the same time, I had to listen to that poor man's bloodcurdling screams until they eventually died right along with him.

I've seen the world blow up like a volcano and sprinkle from the heavens like ashes.

There are no happy endings. There is no beauty.

It's a grim dark place that sucks out your insides, feeding on your essence. The world chains you to down to its cracked and broken and rotting surface, allowing the infected souls that inhabit it to eat you alive.

Sometimes I can see the appeal in Trevor thinking that survival instincts are paramount. Without them, death is imminent.

I can feel Trevor's eyes on me from across the room. He's staring. I meet his gaze, his sapphire eyes are filled with a love so pure that it melts me. All I can do is smile at him, my eyes filled with the same love and warmth as his. He puckers his full lips, blowing me a soft kiss. I catch the kiss in my palm, admire it for a second or two then place it against my lips. After that, I zip my duffle, tossing it onto the floor with the others. I love Trevor more than anything, but my memories of the past are things I won't let anyone take away from me.

Not even him.

Later that night, I lie in bed facing Trevor. A strange feeling settles in the pit of my stomach when I think about my last night in this house. My stomach churns and twists and I swallow the bile rising up the back of my throat. Trevor looks at me with a crease in his eyebrows, worried. "Are you okay, Mara?"

I exhale as my stomach settles down. "I'm fine. Just a little nervous about tomorrow."

"What's there to be nervous about?" His voice goes up an octave.

"The slight chance that we might not make it to our new home."

He kisses the tip of my nose. "Don't worry, baby. The morning is a time when the infected aren't usually out. They don't come out until early afternoon."

"That's good to know then."

Our room is pitch black, but I can see the outline of his heart-shaped face so clearly. I squint as more of his features come into focus. His jaw muscles tighten then relax as the dimples rise up in his cheeks. He's smiling and suddenly I feel the pull of my own lips turning up, smiling in return.

Trevor traces the outline of my lips with his forefinger. His touch sears through me, burns me, and heats me to the core. "What are you thinking about?" he asks, his deep voice hushed. If the room was full of light, he wouldn't even need to ask. He'd notice my furrowed brow and scrunched up nose and know exactly what I'm thinking.

And I'm about thinking so many things. I'm thinking about him. My parents. The infected, blistering world. I'm thinking about how we're going to make it to our new home tomorrow in one piece – if we make it at all. But I don't tell him any of that. If I did, he'd scold me, tell me to turn off my brain, tell me to relax. On top of that, he worries when I worry and I need him to stay calm. I need him to stay focused. So, I let out a soft sigh and say, "Nothing."

"Are you sure?" He's prying, trying to be certain. He's trying to read me by the tone of my voice.

"Yes," I reply with force, hoping that he doesn't notice the trembling of my voice.

He doesn't. He slides his hand over the small of my back, pulling me closer. He envelops me in his arms as I place my head against his bare chest, listening to the gentle strum of his heartbeat. Pounding then thumping. Pounding then thumping. Pounding then thumping. I close my eyes and exhale. Trevor is a drummer. He twirls the sticks around his finger before beating them down against the surface while I listen to the best solo that I've heard in my entire life.

I feel like his heart is speaking to me directly. It's telling me that it's never beat this wild for anybody else.

I receive a kiss on the temple, and Trevor tangles his fingers through my strands of black hair. "You know, I've loved you since the first time I saw you in the high school cafeteria. Have I ever told you that?"

"No," I say with a laugh. "I thought you had it bad for blonde bimbos like Stacia Frost." Frost is definitely the perfect name for Stacia. That bitch was icy to the core. Of course, he knows that I'm lying and just playing along with him. He's told me this story at least a dozen times since we've been together.

"Stacia?" His voice hikes and I can see his perfect smile gleaming in the dark. "You've got it all wrong, love. You know that I'm a sucker for brunettes." He pauses for a moment then goes on, "You sat there with a mischievous glint in your eye, a hint of pink in your cheeks. I was enthralled with one single glance."

"Mischievous, please," I huff. "I was flustered and intimidated. The rumor was that you just broke out of juvie."

Trevor's deep beautiful laugh fills the quiet room, swelling in my heart. I hope it stays there forever. His laugh is melodic and reminds me of the Philharmonic giving a concert in Central Park. "Anyway," he continues. "There was something timid, yet radiantly beautiful about you. And when I gazed into your Hershey Kiss eyes, I knew I was done for. I had to make you mine or I'd die trying."

"You didn't have to try very hard."

"But I was a nervous wreck."

"You didn't seem like it," I reply with a grin. I replay the flashback of him, rolling up to me on his motorcycle, that bright sunny day after school. The first time he asked me out he didn't seem nervous at all. He seemed calm and suave, cocky and self-assured.

"But I was," he insists. "You have always been too beautiful and too good for a grease monkey like me."

I doubt that – if anything, it's the other way around. He's too beautiful and too good for me. I'm selfish; I don't try to be, but sometimes I just am. He's the most selfless, genuine, and caring man I've ever met. He gave up his dreams for me, dropped everything and picked up and moved to Boston for me. He's done everything he can to protect me and put my feelings first. And I know now more than ever that I'm the one that doesn't deserve him.

I am not selfless. I am not brave. And I'm not sure if I'd ever do some of the things that Trevor has done for me. But one thing I do know; my love for him is never-ending. It stretches on for the lengths of eternity. And another thing I know is that I'd die for that love because I'm too selfish to go on living in a world without it. "Trevor?"

"Yes, love."

"Do you think we'll make it through this?"

"This?"

"You know, the outbreak. Surviving amongst the infected."

"There are some days when I think that we'll make it a hundred percent and then there are some days when I think we're bound to end up with our bones being picked clean."

"I'm glad that one of us is sort of optimistic."

"You have a lot of doubts?" There's a questioning tone to his voice.

"Some." More than some. Fear and worry lurk inside of me every day. It feels like with every new day there is someone else dying, someone else bring turned or eaten. The only things we have to look forward to are living or dying. And sometimes that is a lot to handle.

"Don't let doubt eat you alive, Mara," Trevor whispers into my ear. "Doubt is a word for cowards."

I want to scream at him.

Set off fireworks.

Blare sirens.

I want to make a ruckus just so he'll get the picture. I *am* a coward. I'm the quiet girl in the back of the class who never speaks up when bullies make fun of me. I'm the person that keeps my mouth shut when I've seen someone does something wrong. I often question why Trevor would love someone like me in the first place. Doesn't he want someone like him? Doesn't he want someone who is brave and honest and true?

"We have each other, Mara. That's all we need to make it through this. We can make it through anything together. We can accomplish anything together." He kisses both of my eyelids. "We should sleep. Tomorrow is going to be a strenuous day."

But I can't sleep. As Trevor drifts off, and his light snoring fills up every part of me, I stare up at the ceiling. White blurs in my vision and I think about what he just said, "We have each other, Mara. That's all we need."

I know that's how I used to feel. I used to feel like I never needed anything, but him. That all changed. Things are different now. The world is different now.

And the last thought that plants itself in my mind before I drift off to sleep is that I hope he's right.

Chapter FOURTEEN

Before

I linger behind Trevor, and watch him.

He's leaning over the metal railing that surrounds the harbor. His leather jacket is folded over the railing next to him, showing the wife-beater he wore beneath it.

I can't believe he just showed up here.

I thought we were over.

Done.

Finished.

I thought that I would have to start imagining my life without him. I thought that I would have to start planning a future without him. It's true that three weeks isn't a long time apart, but still. He never called, never texted. All of sudden, I heard a knock on my apartment door, and he was standing there, his shoulder up against the door frame. Then he said, "So this breakup thing kind of sucks," he paused and went on, "you were right love, I can fix cars anywhere."

If he had any other words, I didn't give him the opportunity to speak them. I almost immediately flung myself into his arms hoping that he would catch me and keep me forever. "I don't ever want to do that again," I told him, my voice thick with emotion.

"Me neither, love. Me neither."

There would be time to discuss the living situation later. What we really needed was some time for ourselves. I suggested that we walk down to the harbor since it wasn't too far from where I lived.

It's a beautiful day out. The sun is beaming down from the heavens, kissing my skin, and leaving white flecks against the blue water in front of us. The temperature is in the mid-eighties, but the wind whipping through the air makes it a little bit chillier. A gust whips through my hair, and I close my eyes inhaling the scent – salt and fresh linens.

I open my eyes when Trevor shifts against the railing, letting out a soft sigh. The muscles in his bicep clench, and I creep toward him slowly. He tenses up when I wrap my hands around his waist. "Like I always say," he murmurs, "Sneaky, sneaky."

I laugh softly, inhale deeply, and rest my head against his back. The smell of dryer sheets, and his own personal body fragrance wafts up my nostrils. I revel in it, wishing that I could plaster it on my skin. "I missed you so much," I tell him.

That is not a lie.

I missed him so much that my bones ached for him.

I missed him so much that my heart wept for him.

I missed him so much that I imagined that he was here even though he wasn't.

During the first week of our break up, I woke up every night crying so hard that I was screaming. The pain pumping through my body was constant. Sometimes it even felt like someone had just taken a metal hook and rammed it through my heart. There was a hole there. A huge, gaping bleeding hole. A hole that I didn't think would ever heal.

He lifts his arm, sweeping me underneath his shoulder. His fingertips trail down the length of my body, stopping at my waist. His fingers play with the frayed edge of my grey tank top, brushing gently against my skin, bringing out a fresh assortment of goosebumps. Then he brings my right hand to his mouth, turns my wrist up, and kisses it. "I missed you too. A lot."

I face the busy port as he releases my wrist. I gaze out into the choppy, blue waters, watching the small boats. They putter along, smoke unfurling from their silver cylindrical chimneys as they make their way to the docks. I can feel Trevor's eyes on me. He's studying me like he's a biologist with a slide under his microscope. I meet his gaze, a smile pulling on the corners of my mouth. "What?"

He flashes me a brilliant smile in return, and my heart constricts in my chest, then starts hammering. Butterflies swim in my stomach, and my cheeks scorch as my body heat rises. I wonder if this feeling will ever go away. I wonder if our relationship will ever turn into a hum drum or boring one or if my desire for him to touch me, kiss me, and love me will ever stay the same.

It's been almost four years and every time I see him, I feel like I'm staring into his eyes for the first time. I become that shy, quiet girl in the cafeteria all over again. I knew it then like I know it now - that he was and always will be the one for me. From the beginning, even though we've had our fair share of ups and downs, I knew our love was different. Something special. Something beautiful, pure, and joyous. It was the kind of love that people wrote books about. I know now more than ever that that kind of love doesn't fade. It only burns brighter as the years pass by.

Trevor squeezes me tighter, and I tilt my chin up as he places a soft, sensual kiss on my lips. "Tell me what you're thinking about."

I'm thinking about how much I love him, and how my world was on pause until he came back to me. More than anything, I'm thinking about how this moment is one of the most perfect moments that I've ever had in my entire life, and I hope that I remember it forever. But I don't tell him that. Instead I say, "You."

He squeezes me, kissing the top of my head. "And I you. Always."

I place my head against his chest, trailing my fingers over his chiseled abs. His heart thumps rhythmically like a song orchestrated just for me, and for a moment I say nothing and just listen to it. When I finally speak up I ask, "Trevor, do you think you'll be happy here?"

He grins, and chuckles, staring deep into my brown eyes. "Where did that come from?"

I bite my lip, and shake my head. "I don't know, I just…." I struggle to get the words out. "I just…I'd just hate to think that you gave up everything you ever wanted because of me." I look away from him, my eyes gravitating toward the pavement.

Trevor gently grabs my face, and moves my head up to face him. "Look at me, Samara." I slowly lift my eyes from the ground, and his blue eyes pierce my heart and captivate my soul. "I want to be here. You were right, I can fix cars anywhere and wherever you are is where I want to be. Don't ever think that I won't be happy here. Seeing you today, well, I've never been happier in my entire life." He closes his eyes for a second, exhaling with a creased brow. "Besides, I didn't give up anything to be here. Nothing important anyway. You're the only thing that's important to me. I love you."

I can't help the overwhelming flood of emotion that's tearing through my insides. "I love you too."

Wetness trickles down my cheeks. Trevor leans down, trailing his thumb beneath my eyes, wiping my tears away. "No crying."

A weak smile curls on my lips. "I'm sorry." I shake my head, and laugh, sucking back the rest of my tears. Enough of the water works. "Let's enjoy the rest of today, shall we?"

Trevor flashed me his mega-watt smile. "I would love nothing more." Both of us face the port, watching the tiny boats crawling across the choppy sea. "This is really something, Samara."

"It's beautiful, isn't it?"

"Yeah," he agrees.

"You know, we could make this our spot."

He cocks an eyebrow. "Our spot?"

"Yeah. We could make it a ritual. We could come here every week."

Trevor purses his lips and nods. "I like that idea."

Seagulls flap their wings, belching out caws and squeals as they sail over the powdery blue horizon. Trevor slides his hand into the back pocket of my jeans as I rest my head against one of his pecs. We stay like that for a while, wrapped in each other's arms, watching the action unfolding beneath us.

That's the thing about Trevor and me. We could be anywhere; on another continent, on a raft stranded out in the middle of the ocean or even on Mars and we wouldn't need anything. We wouldn't need words. We wouldn't need an agenda to keep ourselves entertained.

No. All Trevor and I really want or need is each other.

Chapter FIFTEEN

After

An unsettling silence dangles in the air. Trevor is behind me, pushing his bike. I glance at him warily over my shoulder. We've been walking for about an hour and a half, but it feels like we've been walking for years. I wish that we could speed up this process; the truth is I'm a frightened ball of nerves walking to a faraway location in a world full of rot and decay.

We walk past the harbor, a spot that used to remind me of all things that are beautiful. Now as I stare out into the blue waters, all I see are festering corpses floating on top of the water. I don't know how they ended up in the water, but they are practically baking in the hot sun and the rancid smell of death permeates the air.

They must have fallen over the railing or something. Either that or they walked into the water willingly, the sound of the ocean drawing them in. Aside from the bodies in the water, we haven't seen too many of the infected. When we first left, there were a few clusters of them, lurking in nearby alleys, fighting over pieces of human remains, but other that we haven't seen any.

My spine stiffens when one of the rotting corpses in the water starts moving, wiggling back and forth like a fish. Before I realize it, I'm breathing heavily and my limbs are shaking. Trevor senses my fear, and whispers, "Psst." At first I ignore him, staring out into the ocean of dead and undead bodies until he does it again. "Psst."

I whip my head around so fast I almost give myself whiplash. I wonder if he's trying to joke around with me at a time like this, but the hard look on my face softens when I see him. He's smiling, smiling so brightly I'm convinced he could replace the sun in the sky. "Keep going," he says softly. "We're almost there."

"Really?" I keep my voice hushed too. "It feels like we've been walking for decades."

"Just a few more miles," he tells me. "It's a straight shot down this road. We'll run right into it."

These last few miles might be the longest miles I've ever walked in my life. I keep my eyes straight ahead, determined not to look in any other direction. I tell myself that if I ignore the dilapidated city surrounding me, I can live in some sordid fantasy where the outbreak never happened. I envision Trevor and I walking along this same road, smiles on our faces, fingers entwined as other couples and cars pass us. Trevor tucks a strand of my hair behind my ear, gently nestling his full lips against my ear. I smile to myself hoping that I can live in this fantasy forever. If I die maybe this is what heaven will be like.

I'm so far gone into the illusion that I don't see the giant crack in the road. I trip, falling face first into the black tar.

Trevor slips up, and screams, "Mara!"

Placing my hands flat on the black tar, I try to pick myself up, but my wrists buckle under my weight, so I rest my cheek flat against the ground. A raging bonfire of pain burns in my right hand as I lift it up in front of my face. Great. Freaking great. My scabbed over cut has broken open and red liquid oozes out through my band aid.

I hear the bike crashing to the ground behind me and the loud plodding of footsteps on the pavement. There's about twenty-four feet between us, and Trevor is at my side within seconds, helping me up and examining my hands. He exhales slowly as relief crosses over his masculine features. "Nothing serious, thank God," he says. It might not be anything serious for someone like him. but the burning sensation has worked its way up my arm.

For a minute, all I can hear is Trevor's heavy breathing, and the soft pounding of his heartbeat. The sound puts me at ease. Trevor puts me at ease. At least for a short time. That is until I hear it—the scraping. A familiar scraping, the same sound I heard yesterday when the infected man came onto our porch.

The scraping gets louder and louder. It sounds like there are multiple pairs of feet scarping against the pavement. I can't look behind us because I'm afraid of what I'll see if I do. I'm afraid that if I see it, I'll panic. I know myself well enough to say that I don't handle tense or stressful situations well.

Once when I was about twelve years old my mom fell down the basement steps, and broke her ankle. She lay at the bottom of the steps, pain written across her features, and cried, "Samara! Call 9-1-1!"

But I couldn't. I couldn't move. I panicked, and it felt like every logical thought in my mind had taken a leave of absence. The only thing I could do was stare at my mom, eyes swimming with tears. Of course, I eventually called, but it took me at least twenty minutes to react.

I clutch Trevor's open leather jacket then wrap my hands around his back. He squeezes me tightly, holding me together because I'm about to fall apart. "Trevor," my voice quivers. "We're surrounded aren't we?"

He looks up for a half a second then back at me, nodding. He tips my chin up, placing a gentle kiss on my lips. "Here's what I want you to do, Mara, when I give you the word, I want you to run."

But I can't.

I won't.

He can't make me.

My heart stops beating. Us separating will never be an option. "No," I tell him. "No." Tears spill onto my cheeks. "I know what you want me to do, and I won't do it Trevor, I won't do it." I won't. I won't. I won't.

This is a typical Trevor move. I know him. Sometimes I think I know him better than I know myself, so I know exactly what he's going to try and do. He's going to try and distract the infected people coming at us by drawing them away from me. Their grunts and moans are deafening as they limp closer, and pretty soon that's all I can hear. We're running out of time. Trevor shifts nervously, glancing over his shoulder. The he looks at me, his gaze intense. I look away. I can't look at him. I can't face him. I can't bear the thought of having to leave him. He places his hands on my cheeks. I feel him studying my face. "Mara, look at me."

But I can't. I'm weak. I'm a coward and I'm selfish and I would rather die here in the middle of the street being eaten alive with him than be without him. Trevor shakes his head, tightening his grip on my face. "Mara! Look at me damn it!"

Every tear inside of me spills out on to my cheeks. "Trevor! Please don't make me do this!" I cry out. "Please!"

His breathing is steady. He lowers his voice. "Mara, you have to." In a flash, he shoves a paper into the pocket of my jeans, shoves himself off of me, and screams as loud as he can. There has to be at least five infected people coming toward us. Trevor screams a second time, catching their attention. In unison, they look over at him, limping toward him. I don't get a good look at their faces, but a few of them that have been infected recently - their skin hasn't started to sag yet.

I'm on my feet in seconds, starting after him. "Trevor, no!"

Then in one swift motion, Trevor picks up the Ducati, turns it on, hops on does a 360, and revs up the engine. "Trevor!" I keep yelling for him, but he doesn't acknowledge me. "Trevor, please! Don't do this!" His suicidal actions cut into me. I run for him. I run toward the bike as he does another 360, and all of the infected people moan, wandering toward him.

He stops, facing me dead on, with a fierce look in his eye. "Mara, run!" But I don't listen to him. I keep coming at him. "Mara, quit being stubborn, and run!" he shrieks. I don't think I've ever heard his voice hit such a high note. I don't think I've heard him sound so panicked.

"I won't leave you!"

Pain ripples across his face when he looks at me, but it only lasts for a second, and then the pain is replaced by a brave look in his eye. "Mara, you run to the new place you hear me? I will meet you there, I promise!"

"No!" One by one my organs are shriveling up. I can feel the fluid draining out of me. "Please don't do this!" I'm pathetic, and I don't care. "Trevor!"

Trevor revs up the engine on the bike. "Run to the new place, Mara!" he shouts one last time. Then he reaches into the side of his jeans, pulls out a gun, and shoots a few rounds off into the air. He turns the bike, snatching up one of the duffle bags before speeding off down the road. The infected people hobble after him, a swarm of bees eager to pollenate his flower.

The rumbling engine of the Ducati vibrates in the air, and the moans from the infected people trail behind it as Trevor drives faster, leading them away from me. He disappears around a corner, vanishing from my view.

Chapter SIXTEEN

Before

Trevor walks into my apartment, and on most days, I'm totally eager to hear about his day. What he did, what he accomplished. He's been out and about scouting the area, looking for empty buildings so that he can start up his own garage. His mom's parents had some money set aside for him and his sister, and when they died, they each inherited a small fortune.

Today is not a day where I'm interested to hear about what he's done.

Today is a somber, sad, and heart-wrenching day.

"Hey, Mara, I—" he starts then stops when he sees me.

I'm huddled in a ball on my couch, sobbing hysterically. "Trevor," I croak. My voice cracks with emotion, and my voice quivers.

He takes two giant steps, coming up next to me, sweeping me into his arms. I inhale the smell of new leather, watching as my tears rain down his leather jacket, little streams of heartbreak on a freshly black-topped highway. "What happened, love?" His tone is questioning yet somber.

His voice soothes me, eases my pain, and calms me down. "Grammy died," I sob into his chest. "I can't believe she's gone."

My grandmother and I had a very close relationship. I loved her like she was my own mother, and sometimes it felt like she was. She babysat me my whole life and, up until this last year, I spent two weeks with her every summer. Even though she only lived a few houses down, and it wasn't much of a vacation, it was something that I always looked forward to. During my two weeks with Grammy, we'd bake cookies, work in her garden, and laugh about silly things. Sometimes, we'd take day trips to amusement parks, or the beach, but some of my most favorite experiences happened right under her roof. It was the best time of my childhood.

She wasn't like my parents. My parents were very simplistic, by the book. The had an agenda for everything, but when I went to Grammy's it was nice to just kick back, relax, and be free, even if it was only for a short time. She had a mouth like a sailor, and a zest for life. I always wondered if I'd turn out like her.

Trevor's lips form a straight line, and his brow creases. "Oh, Mara." He brushes my bangs away from my forehead, and kisses me softly. "I'm so sorry. You know I loved Grammy too."

And she loved him.

Every time we'd talk about Trevor, she'd say, "The men that are a little bit rough around the edges are always the ones with the best kind of love inside of them. They have the gentlest hearts."

I'd beam and reply with, "Grammy, you're so right."

Trevor's grandmother died when he was three, so he always enjoyed spending time with mine. He breathes softly into my ear. "Shhh, it's okay love." He squeezes me tighter, kissing my hair. "I don't think Grammy would want to see you like this," he tells me. "She'd want you to be sad, but she'd say that you're young and it's okay to miss her, but only for a little while. Then you should try to move on with your life."

"I know," I cry. "But it's so hard." Especially since it's so fresh. My parents just called me this morning.

"Believe me," he says in a loving tone. "I know how hard it is to lose someone you love. When my grandfather—" His voice cracks, and he hesitates. Trevor was very close to his grandfather, and he died just before we started dating. I wish I could have met him; from what Trevor said about him, it sounded like he was an amazing man. He lied about his age, enlisting in the military at only sixteen to fight in WWII. I've always thought that people like that should be considered heroes. "When my grandfather died, I thought it was the end of the world. I thought that I'd never be able to get over losing him."

I cling to him as we both sit down on the couch and he scoops me up into his lap. I peer up at him, red-eyed and flushed. "What helped you get through it?"

He kisses my temple and sighs. "Something my mom said."

I examine his face carefully. He looks solemn, but there's a layer of wetness glossing his eyes. I can tell that he's trying to keep his emotions at bay. He's also staring at me intensely. It's like he can tell that the pain inside of me is spreading like an infection. It's like he'd prefer to sacrifice himself to the general rather than seeing me suffer. "What did she say?"

He clears his throat, trailing his thumb along my cheek. "She said that people die every day, and that my grandfather was a good man, loved by many. She also said that just because a person dies that doesn't mean the world will stop." He lets out a long breath, placing his head against the couch. "She also said that we had to have hope."

"Hope?" I frown and furrow my brow. "Why hope?"

"Because hope is what gets people through the darkest times of their lives. Hope pushes you forward. Hope gives you strength." I play with the edge of his t-shirt as he goes on. "hope is what reminds you that there is still a future out there for you." His blue eyes probe mine as I meet his gaze. "You have every right to be upset, and you should be. But you have to be able to hope to overcome it. People wouldn't be able to overcome anything without hope."

His words cauterize the gaping hole in my heart. They actually remind me of something that Grammy would say if she were still here. Tears well up in my eyes just thinking about her.

I don't know if I'll ever be able to overcome losing her. She wasn't like my parents. I could talk to her about anything, and she'd always listen intently, never judging.

I stare up at Trevor, admiring the serene look on his face. Thank God he's here. Thank God he has hope because I know that right now, I need all the hope I can get.

Chapter SEVENTEEN

After

I've been walking for a while.

Walking slowly.

Walking aimlessly.

I gave up on running about a mile back. I've never been a runner; I get too winded too easily. I used to be in pretty decent shape when I was dancing, but it's been a while since I've exercised.

I'm delusional.

I'm starting to lose my mind.

I'm even talking to myself, convinced that Trevor has never left.

Yes.

He's not gone.

He's right here next to me.

Aren't you, Trevor?

Aren't you?

The sun is beaming down on me, and I'm sweating profusely. I feel like a frozen water bottle, melting, water pouring down the sides of my plastic casing. I take off my t-shirt, throwing it over my shoulder. "What's that Trevor?" I cackle, letting out a laugh laced with the deepest kind of crazy. "You like it when I show some skin?"

The Trevor in my mind answers back, "Yes." I even imagine his lips against my ear, his hands sliding up my back and over my shoulder before he wraps his strong arms around my chest and pulls me close to him. The illusion feels so real that I swear I can feel the heat from his body radiating onto mine. I can feel his exposed skin on mine and his searing touch scorches me inside and out. And I want it. I want his touch so badly it feels like my bones are brittle and breaking, aching for it. I want him to crush his body into mine, and snap me in half like a twig.

Touch me. Touch me. Touch me. Reality hits when I realize that it's not Trevor's hands that are on me, they are my own. And I can't believe that I even imagined that my hands feel similar to Trevor's because they don't. It's not even close. When I step out of the illusion that I've been living in, it hits me again that Trevor's gone, and I fall apart for what feels like the hundredth time this month.

I have to stop walking. I can't go any further. I plop down on the ground, in the middle of the road, hugging my knees tightly to my chest. My sobs echo, bouncing off the crumbling buildings surrounding me. They pump through my body like a stab of adrenaline shot straight into my heart. I can't breathe. I can't breathe, and I don't want to.

I'm hit with a vision; another perfect memory of life before the outbreak. My grandmother had just passed away, and Trevor had come over to attend the service with my family. When he found me, I was in my old bedroom curled up in a ball on my bed, hysterical.

He made his way over to me in two strides, scooping me up into his arms.

It will be okay, he told me.

She's having a spritzer with God, he said.

He got me through that difficult time with his supportive nature, soothing words, and understanding demeanor. Thinking of that moment gives me hope. Maybe Trevor is out there somewhere and he's okay. He's smart and strong and the ultimate survivalist. I bet he's already made it to our new place and is on the front porch waiting for me. He has to be. He just has to be.

I'm up off the ground in a flash, sprinting, sucking back my tears with that thought in mind. I pick up speed charging forward as a gust of wind blows, and whips through my hair. The wind soothes me. The cool gusts tell me that somehow everything is going to be fine. I should keep running because the longer and faster I run, the closer I'll be to seeing Trevor.

I run for seconds. Minutes. Then somehow it feels like I have been running for days and I'm not sure where I am. Trevor told me that it was a straight shot. I come to a halt in front of a tall, metal linked chain fence with sharp coiled wires lining the top of it. Past the fence is a row of houses, but they look vacant, like they haven't been lived in in years. A soft beeping noise fills my ears. I glance up toward the top of the fence, noticing a timer of some sort. The numbers are red, flashing, and counting down. But what is it counting down to?

Twenty-five minutes and forty-five seconds. Twenty-five minutes and forty-four seconds. I shove my hand into my pocket, removing the piece of paper Trevor gave me. All that's on it is a number, 1945. An address perhaps? My eyes scan the row of houses and sure enough the one at the end of the row on the far right has the numbers 1945 on it.

Gripping onto the fence, I shake it and scream, "Hey!" I shake it harder. "Is anybody out there?"

Less than a second later, a slight buzzing noise fills the air. A gate a few steps down opens slowly. I walk down to the opening, walk right through it, and a few seconds later it snaps shut. Metal against metal bangs loudly. I jump, startled. Pivoting, I walk back over to the gate, and try to pull it open, but it's locked. A second later, I start freaking out. What if Trevor isn't back? How will he be able to get inside? Will someone just open the gate like they did for me? Speaking of that someone, where are they? Do they have someone watching?

"What's going on?" I'm panting and hysterical and I can feel the tears brimming over the edges of my eyes. "Somebody! Can anybody hear me?" There is no one, and the gate still won't open. Defeated, I back away from the gate, walking toward the house that's number matches the one on my paper. Maybe Trevor is inside, but doubt swirls through me as I scan the small, square concrete driveway. The Ducati isn't there.

I storm back over to the gate, barricading me into this little colony. It's almost…it's almost like I've been quarantined. Once I'm inside, I don't think I'm allowed back out. There's a red flashing timer on my side too, and there's only twenty-two minutes left on it. My heart races. My blood pulses. I keep looking at the timer. Something tells me that the timer isn't counting down for no reason. Something tells me that when the time runs out something bad is going to happen.

Something about this place doesn't feel right. I have to get out of here.

I scan the ground quickly looking for an object—anything that might help me break free from this cage that binds me. My eyes stop wandering when I spot a long piece of wood that's almost shaped like a baseball bat. Quickly, I snatch it off the ground, walk over to the gate, and begin whacking the metal handle with it.

My heart speeds ahead like a race car with one more lap until it reaches the finish line. The only thing I can think about is breaking free, and finding Trevor.

After a few minutes of swinging, I'm sweating and grunting and I'm already exhausted, but I still keep swinging. I will get out of here, Trevor. I will find you.

More sweat beads on my forehead and drizzles down my face as perspiration builds up, dampening my bangs, and matting them against my forehead. Something inside of me snaps. I'm like a savage, wild and crazy, screaming at the top of my lungs, swinging several more times before throwing in some kicks as well. I don't care how drained I am. I don't care that every bone and muscle in my body aches. The only thing I can think about—the only worry that has been circling around my head in constant rotation is that Trevor is out there somewhere—dead or alive, but hopefully alive, and I have to find him.

I swear that I hear his deep beautiful voice inside of me, pumping through every part of my body. Swing away, love. Then you'll be able to find me. So I do. I keep swinging and kicking and swinging and kicking then Trevor's voice is replaced with someone else's. But the new voice belongs to a woman, and it's like a faint cry in the distance. "Stop!"

I ignore the voice, convinced it's a figment of my imagination.

A few swings later, and the faint cry gets louder. It's closer too. "Stop hitting the fence!"

I'm so determined to knock down this gate that I don't realize I yell, "No!"

Footsteps plod on the pavement. The chain linked fence jingles like loose change as I connect another swing and toss in a kick. I shriek, so full of frustration and unrelenting pain that it knocks the wind out of my lungs and it feels like I can't take a breath.

My clothes are drenched with sweat. Every limb on my body convulses, sending ripples of pain through my nervous system. But I can't stop swinging. I won't stop swinging. It's the only way out. It's the only way I'll find Trevor.

I whip the makeshift bat over my shoulder, prepared to swing for what feels like the millionth time when it catches on something. I yank on the piece of wood with all of my might, but it's stuck or wedged in between something. Maybe it's caught on part of the fence. No, that can't be right. The fence is in front of me. Twisting around, I tighten my grip on the piece of wood when I see a guy and a girl standing directly behind me. My eyes travel up the wooden bat, stopping at the guy's large hand that's wrapped around the end of it. What's going on? Who are these people? What do they want from me?

The girl is extremely thin with long willowy limbs, and vibrant red hair that is cut into a pixie. She folds her arms across her chest, shaking her head, disappointed. "Newbies," she huffs. "They always freak out when the gate locks."

She studies me with her hazel eyes while the guy with a broad, muscular build, and coal black hair squeezes the end of my wooden bat. "Don't hit the fence," he growls in a deep, raspy voice.

The guy yanks on the bat forcefully, pulling it from my hands. I wince out in pain as the wood drags across my bandaged hands. Seconds later, the pain subsides, but blood pours from the opened cuts, dampening the bandages. Balling my fists, a sudden surge of anger surges through me. There's a flash-flood of emotion traveling inside of me. "Just leave me alone," I snap.

Then I take two steps forward, wrapping my hands around the metal links in the fence. I start climbing.

The girl rolls her eyes, clearly annoyed then sighs. "Just what do you think you're doing?" I don't answer her. I must get out. I have to get out. The girl's soft, feminine voice throbs in my ears. "Cash," she says. "Get her down."

Cash must be the guy. Faster than I can prepare myself to react, he sprints towards me like a bronzed warrior in battle, hops up, and rips me down, clutching my waist tightly as he lands feet first on the ground. He squeezes me tightly, not loosening his grip at all. It's like he's made of metal, locking me down, and chaining me up.

I sneak a peek at him out of the corner of my eye. He hovers over me by a good foot and a half with his jaw clenched and ferocity in his black eyes. He terrifies me. "What do you want me to do with her, Helena?"

The girl named Helena is very pretty, with a smooth ivory complexion, angular jawline, and cat-like eyes. But as she examines me again, I get the impression that she could be deadly if she wanted to be. "Well first you can release her. I don't think she'll try anything crazy again, right—?"

"Samara."

"What a beautiful name." Helena inches closer to me, and places her hand on my shoulder. Her touch is soft, but the way her fingers cup my shoulder tells me that she has power. I tense up. Before I realize it, I feel my whole body shaking. "Calm down, Samara," she commands in a soft voice. "I don't think you want Cash to restrain you again."

I steal a glimpse at Cash who is wearing a hard look, and a malicious grin. He reminds me of a human robot programmed to inflict pain. He cracks his knuckles, a glint of fierceness twinkling in his eyes. I blanch, looking away. Him restraining me, yeah, that's the last thing I want. I can't even look him in the eye. He frightens me more than the infected. "No," I reply fear, laced through my voice. A wad of mucus and saliva forms into a giant lump in my throat. I swallow, hard. "But my boyfriend is still out there, somewhere. We got separated on our way here. I have to find him. He's still human. He hasn't been infected."

Helena shakes her head. "No can do. Sorry, sweets. There's only three minutes left on the timer. Once it goes off, you can't get back out. And your boyfriend can't come in. On top of that, after the time runs out, thousands of volts of electricity pump through the metal, and if anyone touches it they'll be shocked to death."

I'm not even looking at Helena and her pretty face anymore. I'm watching the clock, the red numbers slowly branding themselves into my brain. More than that, I'm praying.

I'm praying that I hear the roaring engine of the Ducati in the next two and a half minutes.

Chapter EIGHTEEN

Before

I'd always assumed that college would be easy compared to high school.

I was wrong.

I've only been in classes for a few weeks, and I already have so much homework that I'm not sure if I'll be able to finish it in the amount of time I was given to complete it.

I lug my bag up the steps to my apartment, listening to the scraping sound it's making as it drags against the carpeted floor. The sound of jingling keys echoes throughout the narrow hall, and I notice Chloe at our door, her back to me. The apartment door swings open. I rush over to her. "Hey, Chlo!" I shout.

"Wait!"

She twists around, a smile curling on her lips. "Hey, you!" Standing on her tip toes, she peers over my shoulder. "I feel like I never see you anymore and we live together. Where's your other half?" she inquires.

"He's out looking for a place to put his shop."

"Yay!" She clasps her hands together, a delighted look on her face. "Now we can have some girl time."

For the next two hours Chloe and I spend some time together catching up on what's going on in each other's lives. She tells me about her crazy class schedule. "Do you believe that I have a class at seven o'clock at night?" she scoffs, rolling her eyes. "I mean geez. I know education is important and everything, but do I really need to be in school for twelve hours a day, three days a week for the whole semester?"

After we talk about our hectic schedules, she asks about Trevor, and how everything is going between us. I tell her that things between us are perfect, as usual. We're going strong and we've never been better. Chloe smiles. She tells me that she's happy that I'm happy. And I am happy. I have never been happier than I am right now.

Honestly, I didn't expect her to be super thrilled about him always being here. But so far, she's been nothing but kind and supportive about it. I mean it's not like she sees him too often or anything. He's always off doing something, and on top of that, she and I have opposite schedules.

"I'm not going to lie," she admits. "Sometimes it gets annoying having him here all the time, but I know how much you love him and I love you." She takes my hand, squeezing it. "You're my best friend. If you want him to be here, I want him to be here."

I smile, and embrace Chloe tightly. I swear, I've lucked out in life. I have an amazing boyfriend, wonderful parents, and a best friend who is heaven sent. What more could a girl ask for?

Chloe pulls out of the hug, holding her hands in her lap. I lean into the couch. folding my legs up into an Indian style position. "So, what about you?"

She scrunches her eyebrows together. "What about me?"

"Is there a special someone in your life?" I ask, pointing at her with a playful smirk on my lips.

"Ha," she snorts and laughs. "The whole relationship in college is going to be a no-go for me. There is way too much male real estate here." Chloe has always been a bit fickle when it comes to the other sex. In high school, she dated around a lot.

We roar with laughter, falling back onto the couch, clutching our sides. I'm laughing so hard that tears slipping out of the corners or my eyes. I curl up into a fetal position, and don't even notice that Trevor is standing next to the couch. His deep voice cuts into mine and Chloe's bout of laughter. "Did I walk into something? Are you two gossiping about me?"

I give him an odd look. Me? Gossip? "No." I try to control the chuckle in my voice.

"Nah," Chloe says as she gets to her feet. She reaches down, and snatches her knapsack from the floor. "You two lovebirds have fun. I'm going to go study."

Trevor flops down next to me as Chloe closes her bedroom

door. He pulls my legs into his lap, massaging my calf muscles. "How was your day?"

I sit up and snuggle into his chest. "Okay, and yours? Did you find the place that you were looking for?"

"There were lots of possibilities. I guess I have some things to think over." Trevor bends over my legs, and grabs the remote from the coffee table. There isn't much to my apartment. The walls are a plain white and the carpet is tan. We don't have any decorations, and the couch is a brown leather sectional. Trevor flicks the television on and there's some breaking news announcement on. "What's this?"

I shrug. "What time is it?"

"Six. It's probably the news."

"Change the channel."

Trevor flips through channel after channel and the same announcement is on every one of them. He stops channel surfing, and sets the remote down. We both watch the screen intensely, then I examine Trevor's face. His blue eyes dart back and forth from my face to the television screen. His full lips have formed a straight line, his jaw clenched.

"Trevor," I glance warily at the television screen then back at him. "What's wrong? What's going on?" I'm not really paying attention to what's on the screen.

Trevor sits up further, his elbows to his knees, and says in a low hoarse tone, "There's been some sort of outbreak."

Chapter NINETEEN

After

There's red. Red everywhere. It's all I can think about. It's all I can see.

Red and silver blurs together, creating a metallic shade of pink, and in seconds the fence and clock are spinning together, whirling around like a cyclone only a few feet in front of me. He's not going to make it. Trevor is not going to make it back before the clock runs out.

Helena says something to me, but I can't hear her. I've tuned her out, and her hand falls from my shoulder as I hit my knees. My hope and positivity are replaced with doubt and fear and the emotions claw at my insides like an eagle with razor sharp talons.

They want me to bleed. They won't be satisfied until I'm a scratched up, shredded bloody mess lying cold on the pavement.

During that second, I think of the first intimate moment that I ever shared with Trevor. I think of the beauty in that moment and how it will always be one of the best memories I have. Trevor was more experienced than me sexually, but that didn't matter to him. He told me I was different. He told me I was special.

I know why I'm different from all of the other girls that he's been with. I know why I'm special. I'm different and special because I have something that all of the other girls didn't.

I have his heart.

I always will.

I swear I can feel it inside of me. I swear I can feel it beating in sync with mine. I look up, and there's fifteen seconds left on the clock. As the beeping from the device echoes in my ears, and tears swell in my bark colored eyes, I hear something else; the faint roar of an engine.

A motorcycle engine.

"Trevor!" I'm on my feet, running along the edge of the fence. "Trevor!"

When I first spotted him, he looked like a black thumbtack in the middle of a map of the world. So small and so far away, but as he speeds closer I can make out his broad outline and the wisps of his golden hair blowing in the wind.

I can't even describe the way I feel because it's too good for words. Trevor speeds up next to me, and smiles. "I told you I'd be back. You miss me?"

"Just get in here!"

He revs up the engine to the bike, and speed toward the gate. Helena is still standing there, making sure that it's open. "Hurry!" she shouts. "You have five seconds!"

Trevor turns off the bike, pushing it through the gate. There are three duffle bags secured to the back of it, and just as he gets the bike through, the timer goes off and the fence goes live, sparking and hissing as electricity flows freely through it.

Helena and Cash greet Trevor. They chit-chat for a few minutes and Cash pats Trevor on the shoulder. Helena and Cash both wave to me before walking off in the opposite direction. "We'll be in touch!" Helena shouts just before she and Cash round the corner.

Before I know it, I'm in Trevor's arms, wrapping my long, willowy legs around his back, kissing him. "Don't ever do that to me again," I say in between kisses. Trevor grips onto the back of my thighs, carrying me a few steps before he starts blanching, and grunting. I hop down off of him, backing away. I eye him, concerned. "Trev, you okay?"

"I'm just a little sore," he tells me. "Nothing to be overly concerned about." He drapes his arm over my shoulder, squeezing me tightly. "So, should we explore our new house?"

I smirk. "How do you know that I didn't explore it already?"

He laughs and I realize how much I have missed it. I was only away from it for about an hour, but still. "Because I know you, and I know you never like to be surprised first."

This is true. I hate doing things first. It doesn't matter if it's being the first person in a buffet line or being the first person to walk out the classroom. I never went first. There are always awkward stares or people whispering. It's just an all-around uncomfortable feeling. Nonetheless, it's an insecurity of mine and Trevor knows it.

He picks up the Ducati, pushing it down the street as we walk to our new home. All of the houses look the same. They're all white with black shutters, and black roofs. The metal numbers 1945 fill my vision as Trevor parks the Ducati, and unloads all of our duffle bags.

We walk up the wooden porch steps. The wood on the porch has been painted black and it smells fresh. I inhale deeply, thankful to be smelling something other than rotting corpses.

Trevor pushes the front door open and we walk inside. I find the light switch on the wall, and turn the lights on. The interior of the house is plain with white walls, hardwood floors, and it's furnished modestly with a tan love-seat and small television. To my left is a small dining room with a fold up table, and two chairs. Trevor walks into the other room and I run my fingers along the white walls. They feel smooth. Something about the feel of them makes me feel like everything is going to be okay. Trevor returns a minute later, and I look at him. "So this is it?"

"Yep." There's a haunting tone to his voice, and he's been acting weird since he got back.

"Trevor, are you sure you're okay?" I walk to him, grip his fingers, and squeeze tightly.

He kisses the top of my head. "Yes, love. I'm fine." He leads me down the hall with a sinful smirk on his lips. "What do you say we check out the bedroom?"

I bite my bottom lip, and gaze at him seductively. "I like that idea."

The bedroom reminds me of the other two rooms I've seen—plain. The bed is covered in a white blanket with a few matching white pillows. There are two brown dressers, one on each side of the room, and a walk-in closet. Don't get me wrong, I'm not complaining. We don't need anything spectacular. All we really need is a bed.

Playfully, I tackle Trevor, and we fall back on the bed laughing. Trevor touches my cheek, and there's a hint of sadness in his eyes. "I missed you so much, Mara. The only thing that got me though today was knowing that I had to get back to you."

"I have to admit that there were a few moments where I didn't think you'd make it. But I shouldn't have thought like that," I tell him. "You never break your promises."

He laughs. "I try."

All of a sudden, I realize how badly I want his hands on me. I roll over, on top of him, inching my fingers up his shirt. I smile, and waves of black fall around my face. Trevor sits up, and tucks my hair behind my ears, and then he places a soft kiss on my cheek. He lies back, and I hover above him, inches away from his lips. All I want is to kiss him, to feel the warmth of his mouth on mine. Teasingly, I trace the outline of his lips with my finger, and he cups his hand around the back of my neck, pulling me closer. I'm an inch away from his mouth and his warm breath that smells of coffee and sweet dreams wafts up my nostrils. "I want you," I whisper.

In a flash he whips me around, pinning me down while examining my face. There's a loving spark in his eye, and a wicked smirk on his lips. "Oh yeah," he whispers into my ear. "You know how I love to give you what you want."

"Hmmm," I moan as he kisses my neck, and nibbles on my ear. I'm drowning in a sea of seductive bliss. I clutch the opening of his leather jacket with both hands and crush my mouth to his. Our kissing intensifies, and I find myself hoping that he'll suffocates me with his kisses like he suffocates me with his love. But then, he pulls out of the kiss, and I sit up slightly disappointed. "Why'd you stop?" I ask with a frown. I'm hot for him, and I'm certain that he feels the same way. Trevor definitely has an appetite when it comes to all carnal urges.

He lies down next to me, and exhales. "I'm just really tired," he says with a yawn. "I think that sleepless night from a few days ago is catching up to me."

"Oh," I say. I'm still a little disappointed that our heated make-out session ended so abruptly, but I want Trevor to feel well. If he feels like he needs to get some sleep, I'll leave him alone so that he can. "Get some sleep then." I get up from the bed, and walk toward the door, pausing to ask him one more time, "Trev, are you sure you're okay?"

"Fine, my love."

I nod. If he says he's okay, I have to believe him, right? I turn off the light, and just as I open the door to leave he says, "Mara."

I linger in the doorway, looking over my shoulder. "Yes, babe."

"Remember when you said you wanted to learn how to fire a gun?"

"Vaguely." I try to think of the moment when I said that, and I remember that it was right after Trevor killed that infected man on our porch. I'm not really sure if I want to know how to fire a weapon. I just said that at the time out of fear. Truthfully, I don't think that I have it inside of me to be able to shoot anyone with one. "Why?"

"Because it's about time you learned how to protect yourself."

"Why now?"

Trevor changes the subject. "Don't worry about it. Just know that tomorrow morning I'm going to teach you how to shoot."

He doesn't say anything else. He rolls over and within seconds I can hear him snoring. An overwhelming sense of fear circles through my gut that maybe there is something more wrong with Trevor than he's letting on.

Chapter
TWENTY

Before

I can't tear my eyes away from the television. In fact, I get up from the couch, sitting down with my legs crossed a few inches away from the screen. "Chloe, get out here!" I shout.

Chloe's door bangs against the wall, and her footsteps pound into the carpet. First, she glares at Trevor, then at me. "What's going on?"

I point to the television screen. "Something bad."

Chloe plops down next to me, pretzeling her legs. I glance warily over my shoulder at Trevor. His face is expressionless and he grabs the remote turning up the volume. I stare at Chloe, her eyes glued to the television screen. "It's some sort of pandemic."

"Wait," I blurt out as a special report sign flashes on the screen.

A newscaster comes on the screen, and all three of us gape at the regal man as he shuffles a stack of papers and puts an earpiece in his ear. "Good evening Boston. I'm Mike Weathers, reporting with more information on the outbreak that occurred two weeks ago." He pauses briefly, touching his earpiece and I assume that he's getting more information. "We've just received word that the number of infected citizens has reached a staggering fifteen thousand."

What?

What?

When did this happen? How could this happen? Why weren't we paying attention?

I turn to Chloe and Trevor. "Have you guys seen this on the news before?"

Both of them shake their heads. Then again, we don't watch much television. Most of our days are jam packed and by the time we all get home it's usually time to crash for the night. Something this catastrophic though, they should have blared sirens, gone door to door. They should have done something other than put it on the nightly news in hopes that we just might see it. Or maybe it's our fault because we've all been so wrapped up in our daily lives that we weren't paying attention.

I choke on a gasp, swallowing hard. "What does this mean?"

Chloe cuts me off with a wave of her hand. I look over my shoulder at Trevor, and he shakes his head, shrugging.

Mike Weathers cuts into my question when he says, "We have the head of the CDC via satellite, Mr. Cole Turner. Hi Cole."

"Hello, Mike."

"Cole, can you tell us what strain of virus this is?"

"All we know is that it attaches to your brain and that it fries the parts of your brain that help you to function normally. There's this incessant hunger for flesh that comes along with it. We found the first person who carried the virus a few weeks ago. We were unable to contain him immediately and because of this he's infected dozens more. Those people have also infected more people. We have been in contact with other states and they have people that have come down with the virus, too. We are trying to gain control of the situation."

"What does this mean for the remaining human population, Cole?" Mike asks.

Cole stays silent.

"Hello, Cole." Mike taps his earpiece. He thinks it's faulty or something. I know better. I'm staring at Cole studying the stumped look on his face and I never thought I would ever see a government official look so lost.

"I'm here, Mike." Cole clears his throat. "We are doing everything we can to keep the situation under control." Cole sighs. "We are doing everything we can to try and find an anecdote."

"They don't have a freaking clue," I blurt out. "Aren't they supposed to know this stuff?"

Trevor hits on the off button on the remote, and the television screen goes black. "Well," he states. "I know two things for sure."

My mouth drops open, and I scrunch up my nose. "And what's that?"

"I know that I'd rather have someone kill me than have to live like that."

"And what's the second thing?"

Trevor runs a hand across his mouth, and he grunts. "That humanity is fucked."

Chapter
TWENTY-ONE

After

The next day Trevor takes me out to our backyard, a small square with a patch of dead grass, and a six-foot cement patio. He takes three old cans that he saved, and lines them up along the metal fence at the edge of the yard. The fence reminds me of the electric fence surrounding the little community except that it's much, much smaller. "Okay," Trevor says walking back toward me. He pulls a gun out of the waistband of his pants, and hands it to me.

I feel strange touching it. The gun is cold and heavy and it's startling to me how something no bigger than a mason jar can be

INFECT ME

so deadly, like a poisonous spider. Don't let the size fool you. "Now," Trevor continues. "Aim for the can in the middle."

My hands are shaking and my palms are sweating as I lift the gun. My forefinger slips against the trigger. I stumble forward, blasting a bullet into the ground. I hop up and down whining, and Trevor shakes his head, letting out a frustrated sigh. "No, Mara. No." He steps up behind me, and slides his hand up the side of my body. I lift up the gun, and aim it, and Trevor positions both of his hands on my arms, steadying me. "Close your eyes and exhale," he instructs. "You have to be calm. I know that shooting a gun for the first time can be nerve-wracking, but staying calm and collected is the key." I loosen up a little bit and roll my head to the left and right. Then I slouch my shoulders the tiniest bit, and sigh. "Better," Trevor whispers, feeling the change in my stance. "Now open your eyes and use that middle can as a focal point. Don't look at anything else. Just focus on the can. You need to shoot that can. That can is an infected person. That can will infect you or eat you."

I twist around, still pointing the gun. "I don't understand why I have to do this." I know I wanted to learn how to protect myself, but why now?

"Hey! Watch where you point that thing!" Trevor snaps, positioning me back toward the fence. "You have to do this because we live in dire times and any day could be your last."

"But the fence surrounding us is an electric fence. It keeps the infected out."

Trevor circles me then stops inches away from my face. "To an extent," he tells me, keeping his hands on my arms. "But that fence is on a timer. From eight in the morning to one in the afternoon, it's turned off and you never know when an infected person might wander through the gate."

"Why do they keep a timer on it then?" If it's supposed to be so safe here I don't know why they shut the fence off at all.

"Because people have to make supply runs during the day, and the most effective way for them to do it is by keeping the fence off for a period of time. Plus, survivors like you and me come here. That's what this place is for. This place is a fortress built for refuge, to try and help surviving humans."

"So, what if an infected person does wander through the gate?"

"The renegades patrolling during that time will shoot them."

"And speaking of Renegades, how do you know the two from yesterday, Helena and Cash?" When they greeted him at the gate they acted like they knew him.

"I met them when I was gathering supplies and scouting a new location for us to live. They told me about this place and that it was safe and they said we had a home here if we wanted it."

I drop the gun to my side, and face him, wearing a sour look. "You're not going to join them, are you?"

"I've thought about it," he says softly.

"Don't, Trevor!" Whenever I think of the renegades, I see their cold emotionless expressions and the way they shoot people in the head like it's nothing. "Promise me."

"Don't worry, Mara. I said I've thought about it. That doesn't mean that I'm going to join them." I spin back around and aim for the can in the middle. Trevor places his hands back on my arms, and I squint my left eye. "Steady. Steady," Trevor breathes into my ear. "Now pull the trigger."

My finger slips over the trigger, and I pull on it as the gun fires, and the bullet sails through the air just skimming the top of the can. "I hit it!" I squeal. "I hit it!"

"Good job, Mara," Trevor says proudly. "Now let's see if you can do it again."

I pause for a moment, kicking a loose piece of rock on the patio. "Trev?"

"Yes, love."

"How did you learn how to fire a gun?" It surprises me that I don't know this about him. Then again, up until these last few months we've never needed to know how to use one.

Trevor shrugs. "I taught myself."

"Really, when?"

"When I was eighteen."

"Why?"

A soft smile pulls at his lips. "You never know when the skill might come in handy."

After several more rounds of shooting, I'm finally starting to get the hang of it. I point the barrel of the gun at the can to my right, pull the trigger, and watch with excitement as the bullet whizzes through the center of the aluminum can, knocking it off the fence. Trevor claps, wearing a smug grin and cups the nape of my neck. He kisses my hair, and whispers, "See, love. I knew you had some fight inside of you."

I think I'm more surprised than he is. I never knew what I was capable of. I never knew that beneath the cowardice and selfishness was a bold person with a bit of strength. And all it took was me shooting off a few rounds to find that person. Maybe I'll like knowing how to fire a weapon after all.

"Why don't we take a break?" Trevor suggests.

"Good idea," I say and Trevor holds out his palm as I place the gun in it. And then he shoves it into his pants.

We walk into the kitchen and I take a can of peaches out of one of the cupboards. There's a knock at the front door, and instinctively I jump. My heart is pounding, my lungs constricting. The sound of the knock reminds me of the way the infected used to pound on our old house at night.

Trevor goes to answer the door and when he returns Helena is with him. I eye her oddly and blurt out, "What are you doing here?" Then I realize the way I said it sounded rude. "I mean what brings you over here?" Helena makes me feel apprehensive, but I assume that that's because I don't know her well enough yet. And part of me thinks that behind her cherub cheeks and doe eyes is someone capable of cruelty.

"Thanks for the warm welcome," she harrumphs, rolling her eyes. "I just came to see how you two were settling in."

"Are you like the welcoming committee or something?" I ask sincerely. Not a hint of rudeness in my tone.

"Kind of," she says. "My father is the commander of the Renegade army." Her eyes flash to Trevor. She examines him slowly, her hazel eyes lingering on his face. The way she's looking at him reminds me of a scientist and the way they study bacteria.

She's examining him closely. A little too closely if you ask me. "I also wanted to talk to Trevor about joining up with us."

I narrow my eyes, shooting Trevor a harsh look. "You did, did you?"

Trevor clears his throat. "I haven't come to any decisions as of yet, but I am thinking over the offer."

Helena exhales, rocking back and forth on her heels. Then she gives Trevor a longing look. "Okay then." She turns to leave, giving me a wary look from over her shoulder. "Bye Samara."

"Bye."

Helena looks at Trevor one last time, and walks out of the house.

My head snaps toward Trevor, and I glance at him, confused. "What was that about?"

Trevor wears a haunted look for a moment then shakes it off. He beams at me as he opens the can of peaches, and hands them to me. I start eating them right out of the can. "Nothing," he tells me. "They're just serious about what they do, I guess, and Helena thinks that I would make a great addition."

"You don't?" I question him with a full mouth.

"It's not an option for me, love."

I swallow the mouthful of peaches, and sigh. "Do you really want to do it? You know, be a Renegade?" If he's holding back because I don't want him to do it, I know it sounds silly, but I don't want to be the reason why he's not doing it.

"When Helena first mentioned it, I thought it might be something that I'd want to do, but now I just don't think it's in the cards for me, babe."

I chew another mouthful of peaches and nod.

Trevor looks up at the clock on the wall. It's almost noon. "You ready to shoot some more cans?"

I swallow the food in my mouth, and my eyes widen. "More?"

Trevor laughs. "Look at you. You think you're a pro after a few hours."

"That's not it," I say. "I just figured that we'd take it one day at a time." I glance at the can then into Trevor's piercing blue eyes. "And you didn't even eat anything."

"I'm not hungry," he says shortly. "And you need to learn as much as you can today."

"Why?" I don't understand this urgency in him. I don't understand why he's pushing this. We have plenty of time to practice.

Trevor walks over to me, grabs my hand, and pulls me through the back door. "Enough questions."

On the patio, he places the gun in my hand. He grabs the three cans that I knocked down, and picks them up. The he jogs to the edge of the yard, placing them on top of the fence. He walks back over to me, urging me to shoot with his eyes. But I don't. I stare at him for a minute, puzzled. Why is he so insistent? What's the urgency? Why do I have to learn how to fire a weapon in one day?

"Well, go on," he says. "Fire away."

I still don't. My arms are locked in place at my sides. It's like they have a mind of their own. They refuse to move.

"Come on, Mara. We don't have all day." There's a hint of annoyance in his voice.

"Trevor, I don't feel like practicing anymore today," I whine. "Can't we just finish this tomorrow?"

He clenches his jaw, and scrunches his eyebrows together. "No." He raises his voice slightly, and it's laced with a hint of anger. "You need to know this."

"But why?" His vagueness is starting to get on my nerves too.

"Because I might not always be around to protect you."

A strangled gasp leaves my throat. "How can you say that?" It's not the protection part that upsets me. I like the fact that he's teaching me how to fend for myself. It's the part when he said he might not always be around. I don't even want to think about living without Trevor. "You're acting crazy. You're talking crazy."

A pained look sweeps across his beautiful face. He closes his eyes briefly, and lets out a long, ragged breath. "I'm not though."

I'm so confused. "I don't understand."

"Come here," Trevor says extending his arms. I start toward him. "But put the gun on the ground first," he says. "Little miss fumble fingers."

"Hey!" I laugh as I place the gun on the ground. "That was only a few times, and it was because I was nervous." I take two strides toward him, and he folds me into his arms. I place my head against his chest.

I'm not looking at his face, but I can hear the smile in his voice. "Right."

"It's true."

157

Trevor clasps his arms around me, holding me tight. It feels like he's got a death grip on me, never wanting to let me go. I'm content with that because I don't want him to. It's not necessarily because I feel safe there. It's because I feel like I am home in his arms. I'm where I belong. Trevor places two fingers under my chin, tilting my head up. He gazes lovingly into my eyes. "Do you know why I love you?" I close my eyes. He kisses each one of my eyelids.

"Because even though you're stubborn and selfish at times, when it comes down to it, you're the most loyal person I've ever known. And even though you're timid and frightened a lot of times, you've never been afraid to fight for what you want or what you believe in."

I search his eyes for answers. Where is he going with this? "Trevor, what is this about?"

He backs away from me. My arms are outstretched like I'm still wrapped up in his warm embrace. I stare at him intensely, puzzled, wearing a frown. "You need to learn how to use that gun in twenty-four hours."

He grabs his shirt by the bottom, and pulls it over his head, putting his back to me. I glance at his peach skin, the flexed, defined muscles in his back. Then my eyes wander up to his right shoulder blade. On the upper portion of his shoulder is a scabbed over bite mark. "Mara," he says slowly.

I have no words.

I have no words.

I feel like my heart has been ripped from my chest, and sliced if half with a meat cleaver. This can't be happening. This isn't real.

"I've been infected Mara," he says. "I've been infected and I'm teaching you how to use that gun so you can kill me with it."

Chapter
TWENTY-TWO

Before

I'm standing in front of my window gawking at the six large Humvees that have just pulled up, parking in front of my apartment complex. Trevor is behind me, and I can see the reflection of his sapphire blue eyes in the glass. Chloe is pacing behind us on the phone, shouting at her mom. I tried calling my parents a few times. The line was dead.

Trevor tried calling his mom and sister as well. No one answered. I hope that they're safe. I hope that they're not going through the same thing as we are.

The news had said that they would be sending people out to investigate things, but they were pretty vague on when they would be coming.

I focus on the streets as men begin to climb out of the Humvees. I've never seen so many men in gas masks. Well, I've never seen a person in a gas mask, period.

Loud, pounding footsteps drill into the stairs, and I twist my body, facing the door. Chloe stops mid-pace, and hangs up the phone. Trevor comes up behind me, gripping onto my shoulders. All three of us are staring at the door. I wonder if Chloe and Trevor are thinking the same thing that I'm thinking. I wonder if they're trying to come up with a plan about how we can keep these people out. Fear crawls up my spine, pooling in the pit of my stomach. I focus on the floor, not even realizing that my entire body is shaking.

Trevor caresses my biceps gently, and places his lips against my ear. "It's okay, baby. Everything is going to be okay." I know he's being sweet, and soothing, but how is any of this okay?

At the very second that I have that thought several men wearing gas masks, camouflage suits, and hard hats barrel through the door. They shove past us, and immediately start going through our belongings. They treat our items like they're dirty rags. They toss them over their shoulders, even breaking a few things.

I lose it when I see a soldier chuck a photo of Trevor and me against the wall, watching in horror as the glass shatters. I worm my way out of Trevor's arms, ignoring his pleas for me to stay put. I yank the man who just discarded one of my treasured items by the shoulder, and the man snarls at me, "Stay back, miss or I'll have to use force!"

I pull my hand back, barking out, "Just who the hell do you think you are? These are our things!"

"Government orders, Miss. The carrier of the virus was found in this area. The CDC thinks that the virus might have been contacted through some contaminated meat. Every home is to be thoroughly inspected, and searched."

"But we are not infected!" This is where I lose it. Go mad. Go crazy. "You ass! The government is wrong! The CDC couldn't even classify the virus! What gives you…"

Trevor cuts me off when he snakes his arm around my waist, embracing me tightly. "Mara, breathe." His warm breath wafts over my ear. I'm trying to calm down. I'm trying to act rationally, but these things that they are just tossing around like they are nothing are important to me. I turn my head, glancing over my shoulder, glaring at Chloe. Out of the two of us, she's normally the one who is outspoken. But now, she's not saying anything. In fact, she's not even watching these men as they ransack our home. Her eyes are lowered and she's staring at a patch of shaggy, brown carpet. I think she's still in shock.

I suck in a deep breath, trying to hold back my tears. The worst part about all of this is that we're still being left in the dark about the pandemic. Typical government move. Act first, answer questions later.

The other soldiers who were searching the other rooms in our apartment storm into the living room. Static from their walkie talkies cuts into the silence and vibrates in my ears. "The back rooms are clean," a tall man on the far left says. There are five men total. I don't pay any attention to what they look like. I don't want to remember anything about them. All I want is for them to leave my apartment, and leave it now. "You finished?" he says to the man in front of me. "We should probably move on to the next one."

Without another word, all five soldiers stampede out of the apartment. A nanosecond later, a muffled scream plummets through the thick plaster walls when they storm into the apartment next door. My body goes limp in Trevor's arms, and I let out a breath that I've been holding for the last couple minutes. Worry is a river running through my stomach. I think about what's going to become of us. What's going to happen to Trevor and me and Chloe? Are those men in uniforms going to come back in and capture us? Are they going to torture us? Run experiments on us?

Or worse…

My body tenses up when I think about it, and Trevor guides me over to the couch. We both sit. I curl up into his arms, resting my head on his chest. The sound of the gentle throb of his heartbeat calms me down. The feel of his soft breath against my hair relaxes me. "The worst is over, love," he reassures me.

Minutes after he says that, sirens howl, and an announcement blaring from the Humvees wafts through the windows. "This is an evacuation! The CDC has declared a global pandemic! Any inhabitants please exit the buildings!"

How could this be happening?

I stare at Trevor, a pleading look in my eyes. I know that he's not going to have the answers I want or need, but I want him to tell me something, anything. "Why didn't they give us much of a warning?" They did inform us that our homes would be searched, but as far as evacuating goes we got nothing.

"You know the government," Trevor scoffs. "Everything is always so hush hush. Especially when it comes to something serious. They figure that if they keep everything on the DL when the time comes it will cause less panic."

I grit my teeth and exhale.

Where will we go?

What will we do?

If the virus has broken out in other states where do they expect us to go?

"Do you think they have safe houses set up for this sort of thing?" I ask Trevor.

He stares at me, a blank expression on his face. "I don't know."

I look up at Trevor beneath my heavy eyelashes, panic pricking tears in my eyes.

The worst is not over.

It's just the beginning.

Chapter
TWENTY-THREE

After

Trevor and I walk into the bedroom. I sit down on the bed as Trevor paces back and forth in front of me. "Stop it, Mara!" he shouts, throwing his hands up into the air out of frustration. "I am not going to bite you! I am not going to infect you!"

"And I'm not going to kill you," I snap, sucking back the tears.

"Wonderful! Just wonderful!" he shouts. He narrows his eyes, stops pacing, and steps closer to me, pointing his finger in my face. "Because now you know you'll have the opportunity to watch Helena and the merry band of Renegades when they come for me. And you'll have the chance to stand by and watch -" He swallows hard, closes his eyes, and points to the spot in the middle of his head right above his eyebrows, "When one of them puts a bullet between my eyes."

Tears well up in my eyes. I do the best I can to hold them back. "Don't say that," my voice shakes. "Don't talk like that."

Trevor exhales. My eyes center on his chest, watching it rise up and down. I swear I can hear the steady thumping of his heart. I know it's only a matter of time before I won't hear it at all anymore.

"Mara, why do you think that Helena was looking at me like that?" Trevor sits down on the bed, wraps his arms around me, and pulls me into his lap. "She knows I'm infected. Renegades are trained to be able to spot the tiniest symptoms. My tired eyes were a dead giveaway. I knew the second that she looked at me today that I couldn't keep it from you anymore." I cry into his shirt, feeling a part of me dying inside. Trevor is my other half. Losing him will be like having my heart pecked out of my chest. "Mara, look at me," he urges.

I can't.

I won't.

Please don't make me.

Please, please, please.

Because I know that if I do, I'll feel like every part of me is breaking apart. I'll become that shattered glass littering the kitchen floor that no one wants to clean up. I know if I do, I'll feel dead already. With every passing second I feel like my grave is almost finished. Just a few more shovels of dirt, and I'll be closer to being buried.

"Please, Mara. Please look at me." I hear the stab of emotion in his voice. It punctures me—deep. I never thought I could hurt this much. I never thought this could happen. "Please, Mara."

Lifting my head slowly, I see the water glistening in his eyes, and more tears stream down my cheeks. "Trevor, I don't even know what to do or say. I thought we had our whole lives. Even in this world, I thought we'd make it through this together. You told me that. You told me we'd make it through this together." I'm not making an accusation, and I'm not angry with him at all. More than anything, I hate myself. This is all my fault. I've lost the man I love because I've always been too frightened to put myself on the line, and he's always been too genuine and loving to let me. The man I've loved since I was fourteen is going to die…

Because of me.

"Tell me how," I cry. "Tell me what happened."

There's a part of me that's trying as hard as I can to deal with this yet at the same time, there's an even bigger part of me that's hoping that this is the most fucked fantasy that I've ever been in. My eyes wander over to the bite mark. The raised brownish scab practically burns my eyes.

I know then in that moment that I'll do what he asks. Or at least try to. When it comes down to it, and I see him, I still don't know if I'll be able to, but I have to try. Trevor has never let me down once, and it's about time that I proved that I'm able to do the same.

Minutes pass by.

Then hours.

Before I can even process it, the day is almost over, and I'm faced with that fact that in hours I'll lose the love of my life forever.

Trevor and I decided that we wanted to spend our last hours together, wrapped in each other's arms talking about all the great moments we've shared. Trevor laughs so hard at one of our most awkward moments that his entire body convulses. "Remember on our second date," he says in between laughs. "We went out to eat and your drink when down the wrong pipe. You choked and it came out your nose."

I let out a short laugh. I'm blushing and I cringe when I think of that moment. "I sprayed soda all over your face. I thought for sure that that would be the last date I ever had with you."

"But you were wrong."

"Yes," I admit. "I was wrong." I couldn't even face him the next day in school. And I was completely and totally speechless when he came up to my locker and asked me to hang out the next weekend. "Apparently being sprayed in the face with soda is some kind of weird fetish you have."

"Nah," he grins. "I thought it was cute that you were nervous."

I try the best I can to not feel like my entire universe is crumbling for Trevor's sake, but it's proving to be more difficult than ever. Every time I look at his face, I feel broken and miserable, a puzzle with pieces that are lost and will never be found.

There's a brief moment of silence. I roll over, staring into Trevor's endless set of blue eyes, and the try the best I can not to cry, but I don't do so well. A tiny tear slips out of the corner of my eye, and trails down my nose. Trevor catches the tear with his fingertip. "You know I'm going to have to leave tomorrow," he says.

"I know," I whimper. "I was just really hoping that this would be a nightmare. I want to wake up tomorrow with you in bed next to me."

"I wish it was a nightmare, Mara. Believe me, nobody wishes that more than me."

"Trevor, how did this happen?" Obviously, I know that he's infected, but he never told me how it happened.

"Right after I left you, I was speeding ahead, gaining distance. I hit a pothole, losing control of my bike. I went flying forward, hitting the ground. One of the infected, he caught up to me. There was a scuffle, and I shot at him, but I missed his head. He was relentless too. He just kept coming and coming and I kept shooting and shooting, but he was quicker than any of the others I've ever went rounds with. He knocked the gun out of my hands. When I finally made it up off the ground, and back over to my bike. I picked the gun up, and just before I hopped on, the man ripped at the back of my jacket and sank his teeth into my shoulder. I knew I should have just taken off right then and there. I should have just kept going, but I couldn't. I had to come back. I had to see you one last time before the change."

Tears pour from my eyes. I cough, choking on the sobs leaving my throat. "I'm glad you did. I'm glad you came back."

Trevor covers me with his arms, holding me close. "So am I."

Since he dropped the bomb on me that he was infected, there's been a constant, painful throbbing in my chest. The pain began as a slight bee sting. Before I could process it, it felt like there was a hive of them swarming around my face, stinging me over and over and over again. The swelling has closed off my throat. The burning and throbbing is unbearable.

And I don't think it will ever go away.

Trevor laughs softly. "Remember when Mike Taylor grabbed your ass?" he asks, changing the subject.

"Kind of." What I remembered the most from that situation was Trevor choke slamming Mike in the cafeteria because of it. And I also remember Trevor getting a three day suspension because of it. "Trev, are you afraid?"

"Of changing?"

I meet his gaze, and nod.

"Yes and no," he replies solemnly. "Yes, because I can't imagine what I'll be like. I mean I can, but I can't. Even though I see the infected all the time, a small part of me thinks that there's no way that I could ever end up like that while at the same time the majority of me knows that that's not true. Does that make sense?"

"Yes." What he's basically saying is that he's in denial. I wish I was in denial. I think that would make him leaving and me having to try and kill him much easier. "And no?" I hint for the other half of his answer.

"No because I know you'll find me before I can cause any harm to anyone. I know you'll do what I've asked you to do."

"I said I would try," I tell him. The truth is that I can't promise anything.

Hours later, Trevor falls asleep. We're still wrapped up in each other's arms, but I can't sleep. I've been fighting off the pull of exhaustion for the last hour. I know when I do fall asleep, I'll wake up tomorrow morning, and he'll be gone. I just can't face it.

My biggest fear is that he'll slip out quietly without saying goodbye to me one last time. Then I think of him out there in the decayed city that's been destroyed by a virus. I think of him going through the change hopeless and alone and it tears me up inside.

He shifts in bed next to me, and I run my fingers though his hair. It's soft and silky and the softness reminds me of his gentleness. Trevor George, a badass with a reputation stole my heart like a robber. And it feels like just as soon as he stole it, he gave it back smashed up into a million pieces. The years we've had suddenly feel like no time at all.

Trevor moans, and rolls over, facing me. His face twitches, and I kiss every inch of it. His eyes, the same set of sapphire eyes that spotted me in the cafeteria on his first day of school. His lips that gave me my first kiss and whispered I love you at every opportunity. His cheeks that became flushed whenever he was angry or frustrated. I kiss all the way over to his right ear, place my lips against it, and whisper, "I love you." My voice cracks, and my eyes water.

He surprises me when he whispers the words back, "I love you too."

The words blast holes through me like shrapnel exploding in my chest. I almost wish that he didn't answer me at all. Hearing him tell me he loves me makes everything worse. I sniffle and exhale and Trevor opens his eyes. "What time is it?" he asks, groggily.

I glimpse at the clock hanging over the door. "Two in the morning."

"Why aren't you sleeping?"

I play with my fingers, swallowing hard. "I can't. I keep thinking that if I don't fall asleep then I won't have to face the morning."

His hand slides down my stomach, and over my thigh. He pulls me closer the hoists himself on top of me, hovering above me. He studies my face, leans down, and smothers my mouth with his. Four years of kissing him, and every one feels just like the first one. My heart races. My insides spark. Butterflies flap their wings in my stomach. Trevor pulls out of the kiss, resting his forehead against mine. "Don't cry for me, Mara."

"I can't help it," I say, crying softly. "We were supposed to have our whole lives, Trevor. We were supposed to have our whole lives."

"I know, but sometimes things happen in life that aren't fair. I've accepted what's going to happen to me, so should you."

"You're not the one who has to kill the only person they've ever loved."

"You don't think I'll try and kill you after the change if you don't kill me first?"

"I don't know." There's still a part of me that thinks that behind the bloodshot eyes and ashy skin and moaning drawl that my Trevor will still be there. He'll still know me. He'll still love me. He won't want to eat me.

"Mara, face reality, would you? We've watched all of our neighbors go through the change. Not one of them has had a sliver of their former selves inside of them. Not one of them."

"But that's them."

"I'm not different, Mara. I'll be just like them."

His words echo in my ears. They throb. They pulsate. I can feel them working their way up my canals, rattling in my brain. And as much as I don't want them to be true, I know that they are. This is the last time that I'll ever see the Trevor I know and love. The next time I see him who knows what he'll be like.

I sit up, grazing my fingertips over his flexed arms before taking his face in my hands. I stare deeply and lovingly into his eyes and say, "Be with me. Please. One last time."

He knows exactly what I mean. He lunges for my mouth and falls on top of me. Being with him like this is so intimate and so, so beautiful. I don't want to forget how it makes me feel. I don't want to forget that he makes me feel whole because I know when tomorrow comes I'll be an endless abyss of emptiness.

His hands are everywhere; nestled in the crook of my hip, on my stomach, in my hair. He clutches my thigh, and grips it, digging his fingertips into it. His teeth graze my earlobe. I let out a soft moan. Tears swell up in my eyes, and I turn my head to the side as he presses into me. I'm falling apart, losing my mind. There's an emotional hurricane unfurling inside of me. The only thing I can do is pray for sunshine. Trevor's short, raspy breaths fill my ears as he nuzzles his chin into the crook of my neck.

Hold me now, love.

Caress me deeply.

Make me remember this moment forever.

I can't hold my tears back anymore, and my chest heaves and vibrates. Trevor stops moving, brushing a strand of black hair off my face. "Mara." His lips flutter gently over of mine. "You've been my one and only. I've never loved anyone else the way I've loved you. I can die happily knowing that."

I'm glad that he's content with the way he's going to die because if he wasn't, I think this would be even more difficult. But I know that even if he wasn't content with his death, he'd never come out and admit it. He's the 'I'll suffer in silence type'.

One time, when we first started dating I asked him, "So what's your story, Trevor George?"

He smirked, cocking his head to the side. "My story?"

"Yeah, your story." I laughed. "After the first few weeks of school, you rode into the school parking lot on a Ducati and walked through the doors with a confident swagger and a sexy smile that made most of the girls in school go weak at the knees."

He laughed. "Ha!" He enveloped me in his arms, and pulled me to his chest. "All of the girls or just you?"

"No," I said confidently. "All of them." The first few days of school I stood in the hall amongst those girls and eavesdropped on their whispers and giggles. They all said something along the lines of…

He's so hot.

Oh my God.

Have you seen his bike?

"Do you know why I like you, Samara?" he asked me.

"Why?" Honestly, I wanted to know the answer to that too. There were prettier girls in school, girls that weren't so shy. There were girls that were more outgoing and fun. I wasn't one of those girls. The library and ballet was the extent of what I did for fun. If anyone actually thought that was fun.

"Because I can be myself with you. I don't have to pretend. I don't have to hide. And because I trust you."

Trust in a relationship is key. Trevor has never broken mine even though I'm sure he's had plenty of opportunities. But still, he's never cheated, and he's never lied and neither have I. We've been together for so long now that I'm certain that both of us would be able to tell if the other one is lying.

I snap out of my reverie when Trevor sits upright, pulling me into his lap. He squeezes me tightly. My lips brush against his. I taste his breath. It tastes sweet - like being in love for the first time.

There are certain things I know about myself that I cannot change. I am not particularly beautiful. I have plain features; black hair with muddy brown eyes, thin stick of gum lips, a medium sized nose that slopes up the tiniest bit. I have character flaws too. I tend to be lazy at times. If a situation gets too hard, I tend to give up. I throw a fit if I don't get my own way, and

I'm extremely stubborn. There is nothing about me that's perfect. Because I am normal. I am an ordinary girl, and ordinary girl who has been infected by love since she was fourteen years old. A love I thought that I would have my whole life.

Trevor, my love, my life.

That is the last thing on my mind before I drift into the world where dreams are made.

When I wake up naked in my bed, tangled in a mess of sheets alone it hits me that that love is gone and never coming back. I bolt upright, eyeing the clock. Two minutes. Two minutes until the electric fence shuts off. Two minutes to see my love one last time.

I don't even bother getting dressed. Frantically, with trembling fingers, I mummify myself in the sheet, and dash to the front door.

Outside, my lungs refuse to work. They're on lockdown. I stop at the edge of the porch, and notice Trevor pacing in front of the gate. "Trevor!" I sprint down the steps as fast as I can, but just before I reach him he slips through the opening and takes off running. "No, Trevor! Don't do this!" I grip onto the fence, and my knees buckle sinking to the ground. The metal feels cold beneath my fingers. Cold and dead like my heart. "Come back! Don't do this! Please!" I fold myself in half, and fight for air, willing myself to breathe normally. But my lungs won't work and I feel like I'm choking on the air I'm inhaling. I'm shaking, screaming out in pain, lost in a world of heartache and misery. "TREVOR!" Please come back. Please.

"Mara," he whispers. For a moment, I swear I'm imagining his voice then I lift my head abruptly, and he's above me hanging onto the fence.

I stand uneasily, using the fence to steady myself. I hug the sheet to my chest with my arms. "Stay. Don't leave."

"You know I have to," he says. "I have to leave before the renegades come for me." Trevor backs away from the fence slowly, placing his hand over his heart. I can see that he's fighting an internal struggle to keep from showing emotion. His lips are pursed. His eyebrows are furrowed. He's doing everything he possibly can to hold himself together. Then he closes his eyes briefly, exhales, and meets my gaze, his eyes searing into mine. "My one and only, Mara," he says, his voice cracking. "Remember that."

And then he takes off, running.

Chapter
TWENTY-FOUR

Before

The halls in my apartment complex are packed with bodies. We're like a herd of cattle being led into a corral. Every time we turn a corner there are more bodies coming at us and filling up the narrow space even more.

I'm behind Trevor, gripping onto his hand. Chloe is behind me gripping onto mine. People are pushing. People are screaming. Sirens howling from the Humvees outside are filling up the confined space, and vibrating in my head. The hall is sweltering, and the musky scent of perspiration permeates the air.

I wish they could turn the screams off. I wish I was deaf. More than anything, I wish I had some answers.

Trevor is pushing on the guy in front of him. We're moving, but slowly, and I feel like he needs to start barreling himself into people so that we have a chance to make it out of here. If anymore bodies spill into the hallway, I'd say our chances are slim.

I glimpse over my shoulder. A guy around my age stumbles, and falls. None of the people stop to help him. His shrill, agonized screams ring out amongst the panic as he's trampled.

Reaching out, I keep a tight grip on Trevor's hand as I grab the guys elbow and help him to his feet. His face, stricken with fear relaxes as he gets to his feet. He nods in thanks, putting his back to the wall across from me. I feel better seeing that he hasn't been severely hurt.

This is a mess. First our homes are being torn apart, now this? I don't understand.

What could the government be up to? An uneasy feeling swirls through my gut that tells me exactly what I've feared. They have no control over the situation. It's become a disaster, a global catastrophe. That's why everything is being kept a secret. It's all hush hush. Don't warn anybody.

Trevor's eyes meet mine. He's shouting something at me, but I can't hear him over all of the commotion. I'm squinting, trying to read his lips, but I can't make out what he's trying to tell me.

All of a sudden, Chloe jolts forward, rams into my back, and I topple over slamming my head into the wall. I let go of her hand and Trevor's, slinking down against the wall. I pull my legs to my chest as a throbbing pain blossoms in my temple. People shove past me, and few of them kick my shins. "Trevor!" I shriek as loudly as I can. "Trevor!" I scramble to my feet, but another body smacks into me and I fall back down.

Using the wall as an anchor, I get to my feet a second time, standing on my tiptoes I try to see if I can spot Trevor or Chloe. I don't see Chloe anywhere, but I can make out Trevor's strands of gold a few feet in front of me.

With will and determination I start barreling into bodies, pushing my way through the sea of people. We're only a few feet away from the door, and I have no idea what's going to be going on in the streets when we get out there. It's not something that I want to face alone. I don't fare well with the unknown. I always like to know what's going to happen, and when it's going to happen so that I can prepare myself for the aftermath of it.

When I finally make it to Trevor, I lace my fingers through his, and he starts pushing hard. He tightens his grip around my fingers, looks over his shoulder at me and says, "When we get out of these doors, I want you to run."

I nod in agreement.

I stay behind him as he pushes his way through a few more people. We make it through the front door, unscathed except for the bump on my head, and a nanosecond later, we start running.

Chapter TWENTY-FIVE

After

I've reached the point where the numbness and emptiness has overpowered everything.

I'm a void.

A waste of space.

I might as well be infected. I might as well be out on the streets, mindless and bloodthirsty, dragging myself along in search of my next meal.

Trevor has only been gone for an hour, and even though I know that he's never coming back, a part of me hopes that he will. Then I mentally curse myself for thinking that. Fuck hope and forget it. I know that hope abandoned me the second Trevor turned his back, and took off running.

A fist pounds into the door, but I ignore it. I managed to pry myself away from the fence and collapsed into the bed, the effort sapping my energy. I stood at that fence hoping, wishing, praying that he'd turn around. I stood there watching him turn into a small dot in the distance and fade into nothing. I stood there clinging to my last shred of hope as reality set in.

Now everything seems senseless and stupid and everything has gone to shit. The once beautiful sun is shit. My safety is shit. And this house is shit.

There are pieces of Trevor everywhere. His black leather jacket is crumpled up into a pile next to the door. His scent, a mixture of sweat and dove soap linger in the air. And he left me a letter, taped to the door under a picture of us. I can't bring myself to read it and I can't bring myself to even look at the picture. It will all be too painful, too real.

The knocks continue at the door and I hear Helena shout, "Open up! We know he's in there!"

But he's not, you moron.

You're too late.

He's gone.

Gone. Gone. Gone.

He's never coming back.

I can hear the wood on the front door cracking as Helena and whoever is with her break it open. Suddenly the whole house is filled with the sound of stomping feet. I don't even bother moving from my spot. I know they'll be in here any minute.

I sit in the center of the bed, Indian style, staring blankly ahead when the bedroom door creaks open. I hear light breathing. It's too soft to be a man. "Hello, Helena," I say mechanically.

"Where is he, Samara?" she asks adamantly. "I'm just asking you out of courtesy, you know. If he's here hiding somewhere we'll find him. You know this."

"I'm not hiding him. He's not here." My own voice echoes in my ears and I never thought I could sound so cold. "Search everything if you want. You won't find him. He's out there somewhere. He's never coming back." I hear the door close. I hear the rustling of paper. Helena's found my letter. It's at that moment that I snap. I go wild, go crazy. And I haven't even bothered to put on clothes. As she tries to pull the letter from the door, I lunge at her, trying to rip the letter and photo from her grasp. "Don't you touch it! It's mine," I scream. I've never been irrational or temperamental, but Helena has sparked a burning rage inside of me, and I can't seem to turn it off. Wrestling her to the ground, I shriek wildly like a lunatic, clawing at her hands. "Give it to me! Give it back!" Helena has the last words my love has ever said to me. Those words are mine. They were meant for me and only me and I'm not going to share them with anybody. I'm not going to let her take that away so I pin her down with my knees, digging them deep into her arms, and snatch the letter from her hand.

Cash stampedes down the hall, ripping me off of her, his thick tree-trunk arm fastened around my waist. Getting up slowly, Helena stares at me, stunned. She examines me, studying me hard. She touches the side of my face, tries to tilt my head to the side, but I flinch, and turn in the opposite direction. I thrash violently, but Cash tightens his grip around my waist almost cutting off my air supply. "Relax, Cash," Helena tells him. "She's not infected. Just heartbroken." There are a few more renegades in the hall. I don't bother to look at their faces. Helena steps away, motioning toward the group, "Move out!" she snaps. "He's not here!"

Cash lowers me to the floor gently, looking at me with pity before he leaves the room, exiting through the front door. I slide my knees to my chest, lowering my head in between them. Helena lingers in the doorway as the rest of the renegades file out. I lift my head up slightly, meeting her gaze. The way she looks at me with sadness glistening in her hazel eyes tells me that she knows how I feel. Then I think for a second that maybe just maybe she knows what it feels like to have loved and lost. That hint of sadness in her eyes fades quickly and is replaced by ferocity. "We'll find him, Mara. We'll find him, and when we do, we'll kill him. That's the way the world is now. It's either we kill them or they kill us."

I drop my head in between my knees again. Tears fall from my eyes making tiny wet spots on the hardwood floor. "You won't kill him," I tell her, my voice full of certainty.

"Excuse me?" She takes a few steps forward and her soft footsteps throb in my ears. "You obviously don't…"

I cut her off quickly. "I know you won't kill him. Do you want to know how I know that?"

Helena doesn't answer.

"I know you won't kill him because I'm going to kill him first."

After Helena leaves, I retreat back to my space on the bed, sitting down in the middle of it, the photo and letter still in my grasp. My fingers are trembling, my heart cracked and broken. My eyes center on the letter. I'm fighting the better half of myself to keep myself from reading it. I set the letter and photo down on the bed, looking to my left. Trevor's spot still looks slept in. The mattress dips down with the imprint of his body. It's at that moment that I'm reminded of everything that I've just lost and I lose it all over again.

I sob.

I shake.

I scream.

Out of fear, and out of pain.

I throw myself down on his spot, inhaling the scent of him. I breathe it in deep, wanting it to remain inside of me forever. Even though the spot is cold, it feels warm to me. It's like my mind is playing tricks on me. Trevor, no, he's not really gone. He's on a supply run. He'll be back any minute.

I press my face into the spot, and scream again. I scream louder and harder and pound my fists into the soft mattress. I'm open.

Exposed.

Broken.

I'm a glass windshield with a tiny sliver of a crack. The crack in me is spreading though. I'll shatter soon. It's only a matter of time.

I've never had my heart broken before so I don't know how long it takes for these things to heal. But the way it seems now, I don't think it ever will. I don't know if I want it to. I don't know if I even want to go on living at all.

I wish the emptiness wasn't swallowing me whole. I wish that I didn't feel like I was drowning in it. I'm stuck at the bottom of a pool with no way to break the surface. My heartbeat dulls and dies down. Slowly. Slowly. Slowly. There's nothing. I've flatlined. I'm dead.

I can't move, nor do I want to. I don't want to eat. I don't want to bathe. I don't even bother dressing myself. How can Trevor just expect me to move on? How can he expect me to pull myself together enough to find him and shoot him when I can't even pick myself up from the bed?

My foot twitches. I move it to the left, skimming it across the letter Trevor left for me. Exhaling, I maneuver myself around until I'm hovering above it. My hands are planted on each side of the letter and turned over photo. White blurs in my eyes. I know I need to read it, but I'm afraid. I'm afraid of what it will say, what it won't say. I'm afraid that if I read it that it will make the emptiness speed even deeper into the core of my soul.

Sliding my fingers over the crumpled photo, I'm hit with a blast of internal strength. We didn't have time to pack our belongings when we first fled the city, but Trevor went back for some our stuff after we moved. This was one of the things I requested along with some other mementos.

My mom took this photo. It's of Trevor and me after my big performance as Clara in The Nutcracker. We're both smiling radiantly looking into each other's eyes. An intense ache pumps through my heart. I clutch my chest, hoping that that might take it away, but it doesn't. It doesn't help at all actually. Not even a little bit.

Thinking of my mom doesn't help either. A strangled gasp gets clogged in my throat when I recall the car ride home from school the day Trevor asked me out.

I had a cheesy grin on my face when I got into the car. Mom gave me an odd look. She was usually pretty good at reading me, but that day I could tell I that I threw her off. "What are you so happy about?" she asked, cheerfully. "Did you do well on a test or something?"

"No," I said softly as I blushed. I dropped my gaze to my fingertips. "A boy asked me out today."

"Oh," she gasped as she turned out of the parking lot. "And I take it that you like this boy?"

"Yes." More than like. I knew that there was something special about Trevor the first time I saw him. He wasn't like the boys my age or even some of the ones in his grade. He was different.

"So, tell me about this boy," she said with a smile. I went over everything. The way he looked. The way he acted. The way he made me feel. I'd always felt comfortable talking to my Mom.

She wasn't the top of mother that would yell at you if you gave her an honest answer.

"He wants me to go out with him on Friday," I told her. "Can I, Mom? Please."

"We'll have to talk about with your father," she said. "But I'm sure that I could do a little persuading in your favor."

We shared a laugh then I dropped the bomb on her. "There's one more thing."

"What's that sweetheart?"

"He doesn't drive a car. He drives a motorcycle."

Her eyes widened for a moment then returned to normal. A soft smile curled on her lips as she rubbed my shoulder. "Well then, that's going to take a lot more persuading on my part."

I touch the picture, and more tears spill onto it. "Mom." I wish I could call her. I wish I knew if she was alive or dead. She would know what to say. She would comfort me. She'd make me feel a little bit better.

My attention shifts to the letter. I can't stop looking at it. Smudges of black ink seep through the black parchment, and as my gaze intensifies, there are portions of it where I can make out some of the characters. I feel like I'm playing an up close and personal version of connect the dots. The letter. This letter has Trevor's last words in it—his last words to me. And I know now that even though it will be painful, I have to read them.

With trembling fingers and a cloudy mind, I flip the letter over and start reading.

Mara,

I thought that this letter would be the best way to tell you that the years that I have spent with you have been the best years of my life. And even though tomorrow will be my last day of living, I have no regrets. I've loved every second that I've spent with you and will hold every beautiful moment and memory we've made close to my heart. I know tomorrow will be hard for you, with what I've asked you to do. And I asked you because I love you, trust you, and respect you. And I truly believe that you are stronger than you think you are. Also, I can't imagine seeing anyone's face but yours when I take my last breath.

I love you. My one, and only.

Love,

Trev

PS- The guns are underneath the floorboards in the kitchen along with the keys to the Ducati. Meet me tomorrow morning at our spot.

For several minutes after I've finished reading it, I stare at the letter, hoping that the words will somehow scorch themselves into my brain. I want the words to stay there, tucked into a corner of my fleshy cranium so that I'll never forget them. A gaping hole of regret spreads inside of me when I think of the last word I said to Trevor. Stay. I said stay and I should have said more.

What I should have done was make my brief conversation with him count. I should have told him that he fills me with a love so beautiful and pure, I'm certain that it's extremely rare. One of a kind. I should have told him that he moved heaven and earth for me, shook the core of me, that a life without him wasn't a life at all. Instead, I said stay and I hate myself for it.

I fold up the letter and tuck it underneath my pillow. I hope I remember this Trevor for the rest of my life. As I pick myself up off the bed, I also hope that the Trevor that I meet tomorrow doesn't have an ounce of the Trevor that I know and love inside of him.

When one becomes infected there is a process that goes along with it, an incubation period of sorts. This is after the infected blood or saliva seeps into the victim's bloodstream. The virus lies dormant in the victim's system for anywhere between forty-eight and seventy-two hours, and after that people change. It's weird. One minute they're completely themselves, the next they snap, becoming something different.

I hope he's a ravenous monster, ready to sink his teeth into me, and rip the flesh away from my bones. I know if he's not the monster I want him to be, the chance of me being able to kill him is going to be slim.

I decide that a shower might calm me down a bit. Or at least make me feel a little better, but in all reality a shower does nothing for a broken heart. In the shower, I cry, I blubber, I wail. I'm hoping that I can cry out every ounce of moisture in my body. I hope the tears disappear down the drain with the water after it's cleansed my skin. But they don't. Every time I think I'm all cried out more tears leave my tear ducts and stream down my cheeks.

Sitting on the floor of the cold tub, I hug my knees to my chest. Whoever came up with the saying 'love hurts' needs to have their head examined. Love doesn't just hurt, love kills. When Trevor left this morning, part of me died. I know Trevor wouldn't want me to be like this. I know he'd want me to try and accept what happened to him, and move on from it. But there is no moving on for me. Without him I am nothing. I'm a heaping pile of waste.

My promise to Trevor constantly gnaws at the back of my mind. The probability of me going through with what I've promised to do isn't very high. Especially because if I do see Trevor, he won't be changed that much physically, even if the virus has already taken its course.

After I finish in the shower, I dry off, get dressed, and make my way to the kitchen. Once there, I look for a floorboard that protrudes a little bit. I'm trying to find where Trevor stashed the weapons. I need to keep myself busy. I need to take my mind off of things. I figure that practicing my shooting might help.

There's a slightly raised floorboard in the back right corner of the kitchen. I make my way over to it, lift it up, pull out a gun, and then I make my way to the backyard. Outside, I line the cans up on the fence, walk to end of the yard, aim, and shoot at the first can.

Surprisingly, the only thing that doesn't rip me in half is practicing my shooting. Instead, it releases some grief and aggression as I fire rounds into the three cans. Then I reach the point where I'm hallucinating.

I aim the forty-five at the middle can, eyes open, trying to keep my hand steady so that the bullet sails right through the mid-section. That's when I hear him.

Steady, love. Keep your hand steady.

I pause purposely, hoping to hear more, letting out a tortured sigh because I swear I can feel his fingertips trailing down my arms. Lowering the gun, I close my eyes. I want him to say more. I need him to say more. But he doesn't. His voice vanishes from me mind, and the mirage of Trevor disappears.

I swallow hard and raise the gun. I tighten my grip on the handle, and with my eyes wide open, I fire at the middle can. As I walk toward the end of the yard, sunlight shines through holes in the aluminum like a homemade kaleidoscope. I stop in front of the cans, hearing Trevor's voice again.

See, I knew you'd get the hang of it, love.

I close my eyes, and inhale. The illusion of him escalates to the next level when I feel the fake Trevor place a soft kiss on my cheek.

I'm so proud of you.

The hours he's been away feel like years. With every passing second I feel like those years stretch on even longer. Soon he'll be gone decades. Then centuries. Before I know it, I'll be an old hag, talking to the made-up version of my one true love.

"She's lost her mind," they'll say. "Who does she think she's talking to?"

Inside, I eat a little bit, but I can't seem to find my appetite. Then I try to find things to do to keep myself busy, to keep my mind off tomorrow. But nothing really occupies my mind long enough for me to forget my promise—my mission. I envision Trevor standing at our spot. He's hanging over the edges of the rails, staring out into the busy harbor. He's lost in thought. Or maybe, he's so wrapped up in the beauty of it that every thought in his mind has dwindled away. I'm gazing at his face. He's lacing his fingers through mine whispering words he once spoke, "This is really something," he told me. "I could do this all day."

That was the thing about Trevor and me. Everything we did was fun, and it didn't matter if we were cleaning or just watching boats. "Me too," I replied to him. "Me too."

The rest of the day passes by in a blur. I don't do much of anything really except practice some more shooting, try to eat a little bit more, and set out everything I'll need for the morning.

Before I know it, it's time for bed, and I'm so scared because that means I'm one step closer to tomorrow, a day that I hoped would never come.

Alone in my bed, Trevor's absence is really hitting me hard. His side of the bed is now cold. The coldness seeps through my pores, leaving me with aching bones and an aching heart. At times, when he slept, he'd toss and turn and eventually his arms would find me. Then he'd hold me until we woke up in the morning. I miss the way his arms feel around me. When I'm in them I feel safe. I lie in bed telling myself that I'll be content with just imagining his arms around me, but that's a filthy bold-faced lie. I am not content. I am miserable and hollow and aching inside.

I cocoon myself in my comforter, and then I smell him. Trevor's scent lingers on the comforter, wafting up my nostrils, unfurling inside of me like a blooming flower. I feel like no matter how bad he wants me to move on after tomorrow, I know I'll never be able to. Dead or alive, Trevor will always be a part of me. He will always be inside of me. He will always have the other half of my broken heart.

And that is the last thought I have, before I cry myself to sleep.

Chapter
TWENTY-SIX

After

During my slumber, I have this dream about Trevor.

He's standing under a canopy of blossoming flowers with his arm outstretched to me. He's beckoning me closer. Telling me to come to him. He's wearing a black suit, his hair has been cut short, and he's smiling at me.

My heart swells at the sight of his beautiful smile. I gasp, so overwhelmed with the want to have his arms around me that the desire squeezes my lungs. I look down at my attire. I'm wearing a royal blue dress, and there's a part of me that's wondering if he has something special planned.

I run to him, shouting his name, anxious to be swept up into his arms. I want and need to feel his lips on mine.

But I don't make it to him.

Suddenly the ground beneath my feet starts cracking. I take two steps backwards as the sound in front of me crumbles away, creating a deep ravine separating the two of us. I reach for him, call for him, but he ignores me. He just keeps on smiling.

"Trevor!" I scream. "Talk to me!"

He says nothing.

All he does is blow me a kiss, takes a few steps forward, and then he jumps right over the edge of the cliff.

I bolt upright in bed, dripping with sweat. Everything would be so much easier if he didn't haunt my dreams too. Panting, I turn my head as sunlight peeks through the slits of the closed blinds. I didn't sleep well last night, but I really didn't expect to. Exhaustion hangs on me, a new, permanent friend.

My eyes gravitate toward the clock. It's seven thirty in the morning. Trevor is probably already at our spot waiting for me. The thought of seeing him—even if it's only for a second—is the only thing that gets me out of bed and going.

The entire time I'm getting ready, I keep telling myself that I can do this. I can do what he's asked me to do. He's gone above and beyond for me in numerous situations, and I can do this for him. I can. I can. I have to.

You can love, the illusion of him tells me. *You can do this. I believe in you.*

Even the fake version of Trevor believes in me. The sad reality of the situation is that the only person who doesn't believe in me is myself.

Even as I continue to tell myself that I'll be able to end Trevor's life, I'm still not sure if I can. Could anybody, even in the worst circumstances, kill the love of their life? It would be difficult, maybe even impossible. When I see him will I be able to keep it together? No. The second I see him I know I'll fall apart. I'll be cracked into pieces all over again and there will be no one to put me together.

After getting ready, I walk into the bedroom, take his letter out from underneath the pillow, kiss it, and shove it into the back pocket of my jeans. I want to remember the words he wrote to me when I see him. I want to remember this part of him if he's already changed.

I make my way into the kitchen, grabbing the gun and keys from the kitchen table. Then I retreat back to the bedroom, and put on Trevor's leather jacket. Wearing it makes me feel closer to him, as stupid as that sounds. Wearing it makes me feel like he's with me, and it will make me feel like he's still part of me even after I do this.

I walk back through the house, making sure that I haven't forgotten anything. I've got the keys in my hand, the gun in my jeans. I stand in the hallway, doing one more sweep with my eyes, and then I start out the front door.

Sunlight beams down from the heavens, hitting Trevor's black leather jacket. The warmth is over-heating me, and I feel like I'm baking, but I can't bring myself to take it off. There's a cool breeze mixing in with the heat from the sun, and when the wind blows, the temperature becomes surprisingly comfortable.

Strands of my hair blow into my face as I speed ahead on the Ducati, and I have to stop for a moment to put my hair up. After I've tucked my hair back into a ponytail, I start the bike back up, and race ahead toward the harbor.

Along the way, I keep my eyes open, scanning the outskirts of the abandoned streets to make sure there are no infected people lurking around the corners, but to my surprise I don't see any. The Ducati engine putters and blasts, and I find it odd that the loud noise hasn't attracted any infected people yet. Perhaps today is my lucky day.

I lean over, keeping my body level, as I whip through an empty alley, trying not to look at the bodies that are piled up on the edges. I hold my breath as the stench from the rotting flesh invades my nose. I do spot a few infected people before zooming out of the alley, but their bodies have to decayed to the point of that all they are is half a corpse dragging themselves along the dirtied blacktop. Their arms are outstretched. Their mouths hang open. They let out tortured moans. I blanch and look away, as the faint outline of the iron rails along the harbor come into view.

When I'm a few feet away from the railing, I glimpse at the horizon. It's bright orange mixed with the yellowish hue from the sun. It's beautiful. It's something I would have liked to witness with Trevor if the situation was different.

I reach the railing, parking the Ducati alongside of it. I scan the long stretch of railing in search of Trevor, but I don't see him. The entire area is abandoned. Normally, the sound of the rushing water attracts the infected. They linger around the edge of it, wandering in circles until something else attracts their attention, but today there is nothing except for seagulls flying above my head belching out caws and squeals.

This spot used to take my breath away. Now it just makes me sick. There are so many bodies in the water that I can barely see any of the ocean. Only tiny slivers of navy blue peek through the mass of death and decay. The smell is more intense too. I lift up the leather jacket, plugging my nose with its interior, wanting to smell Trevor again. Then again, I'm certain that even dog crap would smell better than rotting flesh.

Footsteps thump against the pavement, and as I turn my head my heart explodes in my chest. Trevor hobbles toward me still himself, but not. His steps are slowed, sluggish. His eyes are rimmed in red. The pink coloring has faded from his cheeks. But he hasn't changed yet. He's still Trevor. My Trevor. A pang of hurt whirls through the pit of my stomach as I start toward him, and he coughs up blood into his turned-up palm. "Trevor." My voice cracks. I'm a mess inside. Seeing him like this is too much. Seeing him die like this is too much. I want to die right with him.

The spark of life has faded from his radiant blue eyes. He forces a weak smile. "Mara," he rasps, coughing up more blood. "You came."

I'm fighting hysteria while shaking. I open and close my eyes as tears rain down my face. "You didn't think I would?"

Trevor is feet away from me, hanging over the railing, wheezing as his lungs give out. "I hoped you would, but I knew that this would be difficult for you."

Difficult isn't the right word for this situation. This is impossible. He's too much like himself. I keep telling myself that I have to wait. I have to wait until he changes because there's no way in hell that I can shoot him like this.

He scoots closer to me. "Did you bring it?"

"The gun?"

"Yes."

"Then what are you waiting for?"

"I can't." Every part of me is crumbling. My lip quivers. "Not like this."

"Mara," he coughs out. "Please."

"Not like this!" I cry. "I can't shoot you when you're still you!" My chest heaves up and down accompanied by sobs, and a blossoming pain in my heart. I want to touch him. I need to hold him. I need to let him take his last breath before the change in my arms. "Come here." My voice comes out soft and weak and restrained.

"No," he tells me. "It's too risky. The change is coming, I can feel it."

But I don't care. If this is the last time I'll ever see him, feel him, hear him then I need this. Otherwise, when the time comes I might not be able to pull the trigger.

In a flash, I dash toward him, and pull him close to me. He fights me off at first, struggling, and tries to push me away but he's weak and for once I'm stronger than he is. I hug him tightly, crying, and reach for my gun. All of my fingers twitch. It doesn't matter how hard I try to get a firm grip on the gun, I can't.

Trevor's raspy breaths fill my ears. I have no words. Everything that I want to say is stuck in my throat being held captive by weak nerves and emotion. Placing my head against his chest, I listen to his dulled down heartbeat. When I finally find my voice, I whisper, "Trevor, I don't think I can do this."

"You can. I know you can." His lips are so close to my ear that I can practically feel the moisture from them. My lungs clench. I can't breathe. I don't want to breathe. I want to die in his arms. "I have faith in you, Mara," he tells me.

"Don't," I say softly. I don't know what I was thinking when I agreed to this. I know now more than ever that no matter what I promised him, I can't kill him. No matter what the circumstances are it is damn near impossible to kill someone you really and truly love. "Don't hate me, please."

More tears stream down my cheeks. I clutch onto him as tightly as I can. "Mara," he says weakly. "Nothing you ever do could make me hate you."

"I think you'll change your mind about that in a minute."

"No," he whispers. "Never."

I back away from him, but when I do something happens. He shifts, twists, morphs into something else. His spine goes stiff. The last bit of life fades from his beautiful blues. His expression goes slack, blank. I realize in that moment that my Trevor is gone. There is a new Trevor in his place. The new Trevor moans, tilts his head to the side, and studies me with his lifeless blue eyes. He's the predator, he's starving, and I am his prey.

There's a sliver of optimism inside of me. A love like ours was one of a kind. Maybe he'll remember. He has to remember. He starts toward me, hobble in his step, a frown on his full lips. "Trevor," I plead. "It's me, Mara. I know you're in there. I know you won't hurt me."

He doesn't hear me.

What I'm saying isn't registering in his brain.

He continues coming at me, and I continue backing up until I can't anymore. The iron rail rams into my back, hard. I wince as a few of the bones in my spine crack. Trevor hovers above me, a soulless corpse snapping his teeth at me. Even though he's a soulless corpse, I can't separate him from the Trevor I know and love because there are still parts of him left that the virus didn't change. On top of him still looking partly like himself, his mannerisms are still the same. He's scrunching his eyebrows together like he's done so many times before when he was frustrated. His face is twisted like it normally is when he's trying really hard to complete a task. He's biting his bottom lip like he used right before we—suddenly it's all too much and I do something wild and crazy and desperate.

I latch onto him tight, as tight as I possibly can. I'm squeezing him hoping that this embrace will spark some memory of us inside of him. Then I wait, for seconds, minutes. There's nothing. I'm so confused and torn by hurt that I do the most selfish thing I've ever done. I tilt my head to the side, exposing my bare collar bone, and I let him bite me. Then I reach for my gun, and shoot at him, hitting him in the arm. He staggers backward, stunned by the blast and while he's hobbling backwards I make my escape. I tell myself that I will find him again now that I am infected too.

There are things about myself that I know I cannot change. I know that I am weak, frivolous, and feeble, but at least I have the gall to admit it. I know that I am no one of importance. I am a tiny, impressionable shy girl, trapped in a world of fermented rot and ruin, but at least I have the courage to recognize it.

There are hardly any human beings left in the city, but if there were, I've come to the conclusion that they can view me however they like. They can point fingers, call me a coward. They can tell me I'm co-dependent, tell me I'm useless. I'll tell you what I'll say in return; you can call me whatever you want because I already know most of it. The one thing I won't tolerate is people telling me that I'm stupid or silly for falling in love and making love the center of my universe. For me love is the beat in my heart, the oxygen in my lungs. I need it to live. Trevor is my other half, and I've loved him hopelessly, recklessly, and irrevocably for years, and I don't have the power to deny it.

And lastly, I'd rather be infected with him than live a day without him.

Chapter
TWENTY SEVEN

Now

I have never felt more alone or lost or terrified. It's crazy how the change makes you feel. On top of the agonizing pain from your organs shutting down you feel hopeless and miserable. You exist, but you don't matter. You're just kind of there, an added accessory to a world that's already been obliterated.

Since I've been infected, the other infected people around here leave me alone. It's like something triggers inside of their heads telling them that she's been infected too, you can't eat her. They take one look at me, and hobble off in a different direction.

I'm glad. Most of them frighten me—no—all of them frighten me. Even the ones that still look human. Because they're not human, and I have to remind myself of that every time I see them drag themselves toward a living, breathing person.

He is the only one that doesn't frighten me. Trevor. My love. I've only seen him three times since he bit me, but every time I do I feel like I'm looking at him for the first time just like I did years ago. I feel like if I can get him to look into my eyes he'll know me. He'll see me. He'll recognize me as the girl he loves. But he never looks into my eyes. Every time he looks at my face he scowls with what appears to be such a deep hatred and disgust for me that I swear it makes the infection inside of me spread faster. With every nasty look, he kills me more quickly.

Crimson drips down my face, and I wipe the bloody tears on my dirty jeans. I forgot about the infection turning my tears to blood. I've been trying to avoid crying, but I haven't been too successful. I look down at my pants. There are splotches of red everywhere. I'm a bloody mess.

Forty-eight hours in. There are twenty-four hours left until the change is complete, and I can't bring myself to leave the refuge of the abandoned building that I've been hiding out in.

Renegades have been patrolling the area regularly. I've seen Helena and Cash. I watched from the window as they discovered the Ducati parked against the railing, and sped off on it. They're probably in search of Trevor and possibly me. I don't think they care which one they find first.

Exhaustion is one of the main side effects of the change and for the last forty-eight hours, I feel like I've slept through most of them. I don't have an appetite either. Eating just seems silly now. Soon the only thing I'll want to eat is flesh. Human flesh.

And the thought of that makes me shiver.

Chapter
TWENTY EIGHT

Now

There's a burning in my throat that doesn't die down.

There's an emptiness in my heart that won't fill up.

I open my eyes, and all of the color has faded from everything. Everything is lifeless, dull. I feel like I'm living in a black and white sitcom episode. Getting up, I move with a slowed pace toward the window. Everything is in slow motion. Birds flap their wings up and down with their normal zeal. The wind seeps in through the open window, tousling my hair, but I can barely feel it. It feels like all of senses have been turned off.

The only thing I can't deny, the only thing that I can't ignore, is this undying hunger inside of me. It latches on to my stomach, a parasite devouring me slowly. It's overwhelming and I swear I can feel it through every part of my body. It's in my throat. It's in my mouth. It's even in my ears. I try to speak, but the only thing that comes out is a moan. I try to think, but it feels like a brick wall has been put up inside of my brain. I need to get out of this building. I need to feed this hunger before it eats me alive.

Walking ever so slowly, I make my way out of the building, and onto the street. It is abandoned. Everything is quiet, dead. The vacant buildings loom above me cast with eerie shadows and rows of empty cars line the streets.

I am the only one out here. I move forward sluggishly, uncertain of where I'm going. All I know is that I need food. All I know is that this hunger keeps rising up the back of my throat, and I need something, anything, to sate it.

I pass by an iron railing, making my way to a nearby alley. There are piles of bodies in each corner of the alley, but at the very end of it, I notice something, the half of a human arm. I can smell it from where I'm standing, and the enticing aroma of bitter blood fills my nostrils. This wills me to walk faster. It pushes me harder. I let out a guttural moan as I break out into a half-walk half-jog. It's like seeing part of a human pushes a button in my brain. Nothing else matters. The only thing that matters is eating.

Once I reach the arm, I hover above it, my mouth salivating. The hunger in my stomach intensifies. Suddenly I am no longer this melancholy person; I am a ravenous beast that's about to devour this entire arm, picking my teeth clean with the bones.

Picking it up, I bring it to my lips, biting down on the rough flesh, tearing the meat away from the bone with my teeth. I chew slowly, not tasting any part of it as I start to feel the hunger in my belly ease up. It takes me about thirty minutes to eat the entire arm, and when I'm finished I toss the bone to the side.

Walking back toward the railing, I notice that the hunger inside of me has died down some. It hasn't completely vanished, but it isn't as nearly as overwhelming as it was before. I feel satisfied, but not completely full. I know if the opportunity arose again that I could eat some more.

I make it to the railing. There are few more like me walking around this area in circles, moaning, and hissing as they drag their feet along the pavement. Their clothes are tattered and torn. Their skin is rotting, and hanging from them. They make no attempt to approach me, and I make no attempt to approach them. I find myself wondering if I'll eventually look like them. Dying on the outside and dying on the inside. I look away, hoping that I won't, but I know that's not true.

Pretty soon, I'll be decayed, rotting, and falling apart.

Just like them.

At the railing, I look out into the harbor. I have this vague memory of watching the boats roll into this harbor, but I can't remember who was with me. I can remember his voice though. I can remember the way it used to swell in my ears, and how that I would know it anywhere. I stood right in this very spot, watching the sunset.

It's crazy to me how I can remember little things about my past, but I can't remember how I ended up this way. What happened to me? Was I sick? Did I die? Well, obviously a part of me died, but how?

There's a commotion next to me, but I ignore it still trying to figure out what happened to me. It's almost as if my brain refuses to allow me to think about it. If I could just chip through the barrier inside of it I know that I could come up with the answers I need.

Think. Think. Think.

Something or someone moves beside of me, and I turn my head to see what or who it is. There is a man beside me. He's young. His hair is golden blonde, and his eyes are the prettiest shade of blue that I've ever seen.

He stands at the railing beside me, staring out into the sea of bodies. There's something strangely familiar about him. He scowls at me, and looks away. But if I could just look into his eyes for a second longer maybe I could put some of the missing pieces in my mind together.

Moving closer, I turn my head toward him, willing him to look at me. I feel like I need him to look at me. Look at me, look at me, please. He continues to ignore me so I let out a moan, hoping to get his attention. Then he turns his head. I stare deep into his blue, blue eyes. I know this man. I've seen his face before. I've touched his face before. Closing my eyes, I see him in my mind. He's so beautiful and lively and real.

We continue staring at each other for what feels like hours, and I notice that scowl slowly starts to disappear from his face. Maybe he knows me too. Maybe he remembers.

Then things start coming back to me.

I see him smiling.

I see him kissing me.

I see him mouthing the words I love you.

We loved each other.

Could he be the reason why I'm like this? He has to be. If we know each other then something must have happened to both of us for us to end up this way.

He stares at me harder, and I notice the flash of recognition in his eyes. He remembers me too. My eyes drop to his hands. He has one of them outstretched, palm up. I can remember feeling them on me touch, touch, touching me while I enjoyed every second of it. I remember them in my hair. I remember how the contact of his skin against mine used to make me feel.

It felt wholesome and euphoric and raw and real.

It felt like his hands belonged on my body.

Suddenly I'm hit with this overwhelming sense of emotion. I thought that it would be impossible for me to feel anything when I woke up this morning, but that's not true. My undead heart beats for this man. I loved this man, and still do.

And there are things that I know about love that are astoundingly true.

Love doesn't have a location.

It has no address.

No area code.

It is not a blip on a map.

The only place it really and truly resides is in the heart.

And as I place my hand in his palm, and he closes his fingers around mine I know one thing for sure...

I am home.

Acknowledgments

There's a lot that goes into making a book publishable. First, I'd like to thank my editor and publicist Julie for helping turn this book into something that's readable. Thank you for answering all of my nagging questions and also for what you do for authors. You are awesome.

A big thank you goes out to the team at PhatPuppy Art. You made me a beautiful cover and I will be forever grateful.

Thank you to Cait Greer for formatting this. You're amazing.

Lastly, I'd like to thank my fans. Especially those of you who have stuck by me for the last six years. The last five years have been awful for me, just awful. I'm finally starting to bounce back a little and you can definitely expect to see more books from me in the future.

Other Titles by
LAUREN HAMMOND

He Loves Me He Loves You Not

If I Can't Have You

A Whisper To A Scream

Insanity

White Walls

Beautiful Nightmares

12 Rounds

Just South of Biloxi

The Long Road Home

These Walls That Bind Me

My Sweet Regina

 About the AUTHOR

Lauren Hammond was formerly a literary agent with ADA Management Group. She has been writing since she was a young girl and aspires to be a role model for young writers. She enjoys helping other writers succeed, and spends a lot of time at her local bookstore. She loves to hear from her fans because she believes that without them, she would be nothing.

You can find her here....

Twitter - @NovelistLauren

Facebook - https://www.facebook.com/LaurenHammond-100755776636370/

Goodreads - https://www.goodreads.com/author/show/4115682.Lauren_Hammond

Email - LaurenADAManagement@yahoo.com